Mayhem
in Matlacha

Mayhem in Matlacha

THE THIRD JESSIE MURPHY MYSTERY

jd daniels

SAVVY PRESS
NEW YORK

ISBN: 9781939113306
Library of Congress Cataloging-in-Publication Data:
2016961799

Mayhem in Matlacha: a novel/jd daniels—1st ed.
Matlacha (Florida)—Mystery. 2. Women artists—
Fiction. 3. Stalkers—Florida—Fiction.

Jacket artist: Peg Cullen
Book design by Carrie Peters

Printed in the United States of America

SAVVY PRESS – GAWANUS BOOKS – SAGE SF
PUBLISHERS

Distributed Worldwide
FIRST EDITION

Dedicated to Catfish Bob Burkhart. May he fish the
Matlacha waters forever . . .

PROLOGUE

"Hi, baby girl, let me introduce myself. Don't know why I never done it before. Guess you make me feel shy. My mom tells me that I look like Lynette "Squeaky" Fromme of Charles Manson fame or Vincent Van Gogh who cut off his ear, two people she had been obsessed with for years. That always makes me laugh. I'm a lot more clever than they were. Clever is better than being just smart or talented. Clever means you're like a fox, capable of sneaking up on someone without being detected. I inherited the trait from my dad. There wasn't nobody quieter, or sneakier than him, `cept me of course. He used to say that he hated it that I had to be Top Dog in my classes. Well, I thought, but never dared to tell him, that's too damn bad, cause that's just what I am—Top Dog. I'm your biggest fan, soon to be your only fan."

The form in the gloomy darkness took a step to the left, reached out and caressed a photo on the wall.

"I like your hair like that. It makes you look real sassy. But the cap, it's got to go. Makes you look like a man. And all that sleuthing crap. No way! I know you're the type of woman who strives for perfection. I see that. I ain't seen anyone be more particular than you. Don't you worry, our life will be perfect."

A black and white portrait tacked on the wall over a vase of zinnias was removed.

"Zinnias. Your favorite flower. My favorite flower. Best cut flower. Bar none. Reminds me of the one-acre patch we had growing outside my window when I was a kid. Fell asleep smiling at it. Woke up to it. But hell, when I was twelve I did something to piss off Dad. Can't even remember what it was. Dad put on my favorite CD, took out his clippers and handed them to me. 'Cut them down,'" he yelled. 'When you're done, dig up the roots and prepare the dirt for planting corn tomorrow.' Took me 'til midnight. He thought my sniveling was funny. He was a real mean sucker.

"You know, beautiful, you and me, we're going to have such fun. First, we'll drive to North Carolina. I know this town where we can rent a house real cheap. We'll plow us up a garden plot, raise our own vegetables. Then what we'll do is become parents. Just one rugrat. Two is too much noise. I ain't good with noise. You and me, we'll make real cool parents, nothing like mine or that bitchy grandma of yours."

The mattress squeaked with added weight.

"Of course first I got to get you out of that stinkin` state of Florida. I hate palm trees and shark-infested water more than I hate plastic. And your painting? Sorry, woman, but that's a waste of time. Anyway, we'll be way too busy with the gardening, canning, and chickens. Oh, I forgot to tell you that—we'll have chickens too. Natural, organic, baby girl. That will be our goal. We won't need other people. We'll make our own little kingdom a couple of miles out of town."

Raising the stack of photos, intent, love-struck eyes gazed at the image of the young woman in a bathing suit on a beach. The woman in the photo had just caught a volley ball and her head was thrown back as she laughed.

"There ain't nobody who'll ever love you more than me, Jessie. Nobody. We're soulmates. Destined to be together. Thinking of my life without you is the thing I hate most."

Unlocking the nightstand drawer, long willowy fingers withdrew a bottle and a hypodermic syringe from a rusty tin cookie box long ago salvaged from a visit to the landfill. The state-of-art needle was adjusted and the right flannel shirtsleeve was pushed up. Intense, glittering eyes rested upon the strong forearm and wrist all dotted and scarred with puncture marks. The sharp point was thrust home, the tiny piston pressed down.

The addict smiled.

1

Erratic rain. Threatening funnel-shaped cloud. Flock of ibis obsessing in a field. Towering Queen Palm. In my mind I attempted to paint the shadowy picture on canvas. It was habit, almost as automatic as breathing, this search for subject matter, color, proper lighting, but my brush would not move— once again my imagination eluded me.

I pulled my toner out of my door pocket and raised it to my mouth to play a tune. Sighed and dropped it on the passenger seat beside my plaster of Paris companion, Gar.

Turning back toward the drenched windshield, I tilted my head left and right, giving my neck muscles a restless workout. I'd been in the car since yesterday with only an occasional break. It was now 3 p.m. Hawk, who had once been the coolest boss who ever lived—like EVER, insisted that I break up the long drive by staying in a motel overnight, but I had no intention of doing that. Maybe after I was no longer being . . . Well, just . . . not now.

My monkey ringtone laughed. I gripped the steering wheel tighter, then picked up my phone. Seeing it was one of my Matlacha sidekicks, I slid the bar over.

Gator hardly waited for my "Hey" before he blurted out the news. "Zen's missin`."

"Missing?"

Gator's voice was shrill. "She left this mornin` to go fishin` and no one's seen her since. She told me she'd see me for a mullet sandwich at the Fish House, but she didn't show

4

or send me word. That just ain't like her. She's regular as toast with dippy eggs. We both know that."

Some would think a crusty, sixty-plus kind of guy like Gator wouldn't worry so much, but those folks just didn't know him. He was a worry-wart to the max. It was a good thing he hadn't had children.

"You call the cops?" I asked, rubbing my travel-weary thigh muscles.

"Of course I did, but it ain't been twenty-four hours. They won't do nothin' until then. Twenty-four hours? They've got ta be kiddin'. *Anything* can happen to *anyone* in twenty-four hours."

"So make some calls. Go to her haunts."

"You think I haven't done that? When you gettin' here?"

"I'm in Lee County. Be there within the hour. Have her call me when you find her. She's probably sleeping off a good night."

I dropped my phone on the passenger seat.

I didn't know how much Gator knew about Zen's personal life and I wasn't one to gossip about my friends to other friends, unless, of course I needed to share something for the good of humanity. Grandma Murphy approved of that type of gossip. But I knew for a fact that Zen was having a wee good time with a tourist who wintered in St. James City. Most likely she was dancing between the sheets. Still, the call had me even more on edge. Zen wasn't one to make her friends worry.

I frowned when a dirty white cargo van pulled up way too close for comfort beside me. Through the blackened window I made out the passenger pointing in my direction. The van creeped closer. My frown deepened. I steered my car to the right. "Quit hogging the road," I growled between clenched teeth.

I glanced at Gar. "It's okay. We . . . HEY!" Swirling the wheel, I slid off the highway. Bounced over and through the rain-filled ditch. Tapped the brakes. Slowed the car until I brought it to a stop. Gar leaned to the right, but his head hadn't hit the door. I straightened him.

Behind me, the van with a Colorado license plate that had missed slamming into me by less than a foot hadn't been so lucky. It now rested on its side. I pushed open my door. The driver door of the van snapped open. A hefty man with a two-day old stubble and carrot-red hair that jutted into the weirdest rooster comb I'd ever seen (and I'd seen plenty of weirdo hairdos) lifted himself to safety. I was reminded of my Uncle Bill. The man who never forgot my birthday. My caution button lowered a notch.

"You all right?" I called, stepping away from my car.

Eyes wide, Rooster Comb spit a wad of tobacco on the ground and swiveled as a second head appeared in the toppled van doorway. A gasping woman with long legs and a face covered in a hooded yellow slicker climbed out and dropped to the ground. I walked their way.

The man mumbled something I couldn't hear before his attention shot to the back of the van.

"You idiot." The woman's outburst was interrupted by the lights of an approaching car. She turned her back to me and to the cop cruiser and yanked her hood lower over her face.

The man barked a swear word my grandmother would never let me mutter as I held my nose to protect myself from the stench of a nearby pig operation.

A cop stepped out of his car, slammed the door and started our way. His gait looked familiar. "Everyone okay here?"

Ah, hah. Tobin Peterson, the Lee County cop I refused to go out with last season. I was glad it was overcast and raining, because I'm sure my expression would have given me away. The driver's eyes darted around as he nodded. The woman kept her head down.

"What happened here?" Tobin asked.

"They ran me off the road."

"Hey, Missy, we did no such thing. You ran off all by yourself. You should learn to drive." The man spit out the words one at a time—each spit a wad of tobacco.

Tobin glanced at the driver who looked about as innocent and calm as a shark circling an inflatable boat. "Let's take a look inside the van," he said.

Of course I wondered if he had probable cause. But not so much that I raised the issue. I wanted to see inside the vehicle myself. I hoped whatever was in there was enough to get the two road hogs arrested.

The driver shrugged and walked toward the rear with Tobin following. The woman, face still hidden, took two steps back. On her next step, she grunted and went down on all fours.

I headed for her, but she groaned herself up and sped down the ditch, slipping and falling twice before hand-over-fist reaching the highway. Fascinated, I watched through the rain as her running figure shrunk. Seconds later, a semi coughed to a stop. The passenger door opened wide and the woman climbed in. The truck, more mythical beast than vehicle, roared away, shooting water high into the air. The woman disappeared so fast, I didn't have time to close my mouth as water dripped off the tip of my nose.

I turned toward Tobin and the van's driver and was amazed to see the driver dashing and stumbling through the ditch in the opposite direction, then veering left and heading for a field where cows big as Harleys huddled under a tree.

I hurried to the back of the van. Tobin was lying face down, gun still in holster. A trickle of blood ran down the side of his face. A brick-sized rock lay beside him. I let out a sound, somewhere between what a screech owl or an injured cat might make, and bent to his side. He stirred and moaned.

Lucky for him, the gash wasn't deep. I'd cut myself worse just a week ago with a utility knife while working in a rental unit.

Looking embarrassed, he struggled to his feet, went to the driver side of the van and looked in. "Nothing," he mumbled, more to himself than to me. Stomping to the back, he attempted to open the van, but the door was locked.

Solemn-eyed, he turned to me. "You're soaked. Go back to your car. Help will be here soon. I called this in before I was attacked. You didn't hit your head when you went in the ditch, did you?"

I assured him I hadn't.

He flicked his hand. "Go on, get inside."

I hunched forward to protect myself from the gust of wind and rain that tunneled down the ditch, climbed into my car, peeled off my poncho and tossed it in the back. Heater fan adjusted to high, I thought of Zen, then tapped her phone number. Nothing. Voicemail full. I typed in a text message then scrolled down my contact list. Grandma? No way. Hawk? Gator? Not yet. Wait. Be patient.

Come on, Zen. Call, girl!

A wrecker pulled up and stopped with a thunderous noise and spray of rainwater. Two other cop cruisers and an ambulance followed.

Once the paramedics took my blood pressure and checked my heart they allowed me to convince them that I hadn't hit my head. I hopped out of the ambulance in time to hear Tobin

8

say, "Now that's a bundle of weed. What do you think it's worth?"

2

A half hour later I was back on the highway in the middle of Lee County, this time I tailed a red Prius.

My ringtone went off again.

It was Zen. Thank God, it was Zen. I tapped the speaker icon and placed the phone on the seat.

"Hey, where you been? Gator called worried about you."

"No way!" Zen exclaimed.

"Way!"

"Well, I'll be. Gator using the phone. Hot damn!"

"So?"

Zen confirmed my suspicions. She and her new guy had spent longer together than planned and she sure didn't have Gator in mind when she was with her new man. Go figure.

"I was glad you finally changed your phone number," Zen said. "That has to help."

"Yeah. I admit I don't cringe every time my monkey ringtone laughs anymore."

"I can't believe it took you so long to do that. You being a hotshot sleuth and all."

"Zen, I'm really not a sleuth. I'm a half-ass artist and a property manager."

"Hey, what's got into you? You're one darn good detective and a fine artist. Everyone knows that. Don't short change yourself, woman."

Well, Zen probably had a point. My art *was* selling. I *had* managed to solve two murder cases in Matlacha. Somewhere buried within me was an ability to reason backward, analytically—to figure out which steps led to a result. Still, if I was so good of a detective, why hadn't I been able to figure out who . . .

I changed the subject, telling Zen about the pot being transferred from Colorado. I knew that would get her going. Zen believed pot should be legalized in all states. Once her rant was over, she nailed me with a direct question.

"So, have the cops caught him?"

I let out a puff of air. "No," I said, twisting the bill of my cap to the side of my head.

"You'd think by now they would have him."

"You'd think. But not to worry, he doesn't know I'm coming here."

I hoped.

I hated being reminded about the flower deliveries, heavy breathing phone calls, and unsigned declarations of love that had arrived for the past six months or so. I also had developed the distinct feeling that I was being watched, followed. After alerting the cops in Cambridge, I'd changed my habits: lowered my blinds at night, installed double locks on my doors, walked in a crisscross pattern to destinations, and recently had my phone number changed. It was suggested that I move, but I'd lived in my apartment for five years and the landlord had never raised the rent. Besides, didn't moving give the jerk all the control? So far the only threat was to my mental and emotional state, not to my body. For the hundredth time I looked in the rearview mirror. Were my nerves always on edge? Oh, yeah.

"Well, when will you get here?"

"Be there in half an hour."

"I'll meet you. You at the Bridgewater again?"

"Yep."

11

"See you then. Drive safe."

Not long after, I turned off Burnt Store onto Pine Island Road and felt my shoulders relax. Matlacha was minutes away. Large expanses of water, tropical birds and sea life had a way of calming my nerves. I had no reason to think the stalker knew where I went for the winter months. Very few people in Cambridge knew: Hawk, a couple of women friends—that was it. As far as anyone else was concerned, I could be in Mexico.

Zen was standing at the end of the bridge gazing into the water as I pulled up in front of the blue and yellow building and parked. She waved when she saw me. Her smile was broad. She wore leather sandals, cut-off jeans and a sleeveless gray tank top that highlighted her . . . GOOD GRIEF! . . . now tattooed, beefy upper arms. Her step was more glide than bounce. Her shoulder-length brunette hair swayed under her dark gray cap with the words "Redneck Zen" imprinted above the bill. She moved toward me like some dang mother manatee and pulled me to her in a hug. She smelled like the worst the sea could offer stirred together with major cigarette smoke.

I returned the grip, but there was no way I was going to tell her how much I missed her. Words weren't always necessary. Everyone knows that. I untangled myself. "Hey, you smoking again?"

Zen grinned. "Nah, not me." She winked. "He's talkin' about quittin'."

I inspected her body artwork. "Nice tats. Dragons?"

Zen straightened her shoulders just a stitch. "Dragons, my red-headed friend, are the symbol of dignity and power." As if to proof it, she raised her arms in a muscle-woman stance.

12

So Zen. So very Zen. I wondered if she could sense that I could use some of that power now.

Even though she was thirty pounds overweight, I never heard Zen talk about dieting or complain that she should drop the extra pounds. She was one of those women who was comfortable with how she looked. Zen was direct, fun-loving and, even when she was at her goofiest, I always felt safer when she was around. She'd been given her nickname by a high school boyfriend, the son of a Baptist who was impressed that she kept a Buddha figurine in her bedroom. I liked her from the moment I met her.

She bent over and stuck her head into the passenger window. "Hey, Gar, welcome back. We missed you, guy."

I left her to tell Gar a joke while I went in to get the keys to my efficiency. This was the third season for me to stay at the Bridgewater. Management saved the same room for me. Well, not the first one I had had. After being vandalized a couple of seasons ago, I'd moved out of that one as quick as I could. The second room faced the pass and mangrove islands, not the new bridge.

When I went outside, Zen was still talking to Gar. "He told me he was sick of the inside of that car."

"He isn't the only one. So what's the news?"

"Let's see. The Perfect Cup won the chowder bake-off. Oh, remember Einstein? That rich bitch's pet bird? Guess who adopted him? Big Joe! Can you believe it?"

Actually, I could see the old codger doing just that. I recognized that he was a man of heart the first time he lowered the wrench he was threatening me with and grinned.

"And Gator caught the biggest snook anyone in these parts ever saw and Jay Mann . . ."

I hesitated and glanced back at her over my shoulder.

"Yeah?"

She grimaced. "Sorry, I wasn't planning to bring that up so soon."

Jay and I had been an item at the end of the season last year, but distance and time had been too hard on the relationship. His plans to visit me in Boston never panned out. Jay had once been a businessman who gave that world up to become a damn good sculptor who had far too much pride. He'd refused to contact galleries to show his work, preferring them to come to him. With my encouragement and cajoling, he'd finally taken the step to call a couple of gallery owners and had begun to display in galleries in Matlacha, Cape Coral, and Fort Myers. But with the six-month stretch of time apart and me not being willing to tell him about . . . I finally decided to let our relationship slide.

"Spit it out," I said.

"Okay, well, Jay and Ellie, the new masseuse in town, are hot and heavy."

I blinked rapidly and turned around. "Good for Jay," I said, pushing the key into the lock.

The room looked the same. Safety chain on door. Double bed. Palm tree decorated spread. Small blue wooden table and two chairs under the window with water view. One green easy chair soon to be lit by a white wooden floor lamp shaped like a dolphin. Small fridge near a counter that held the sink. One bank of white cabinets filled with dishes, pots and pans. Tiny electric stove. Bathroom with shower through door near the stove. Chain on door. Home. At least for six months.

"You checked that the chain worked twice, you know."

I shrugged. "Put Gar on the nightstand."

"There you go, bud. Do your job."

14

Like all good gargoyles, it was Gar's specific duty to keep evil out of the apartment. He wasn't always successful, but he did his best. Recently, I needed him to do better.

Soon we had the clothes from my two black canvas suitcases, my case of paints and brushes, my sketch books and pencils, my easels, and the contents of my cooler all hidden away in various appropriate places in the efficiency. The last thing I did was open the drawer of the nightstand and place my iPad inside. I'd had it less than a month.

Inspecting our work, with hands on hips, Zen nodded. "Okay, that's done. Now . . . food. Come on."

"Bert's?"

"Sure. It's All-You-Can-Eat Fish Night. Besides, I'm working now at their gallery. I need to frequent the place even more."

I scrunched my nose and gave Zen a puzzled look. "Did I know about this new job?"

She took my arm. "Just started. But, I'm liking retail. Fun to talk to the tourists."

I did an internal eye roll. Retail? Zen? REALLY?

3

As we strolled, Zen talked about her new squeeze. He was, she assured me, the best lay in Lee County.

In front of Bert's she planted herself behind the dumpster where one of the young, pretty waitresses was having a cigarette.

"Hey, don't get any ideas. You're no longer a smoker, remember?"

Zen stepped close to the waitress. With heads together they whispered for several minutes while I, back to wall, studied cloud shadows and absorbed the sorcery of Matlacha. I smiled a thin smile when the bridge groaned under the weight of vehicles, then coughed a metallic protest.

I inhaled salt air and turned away from the women. It wouldn't be long now. Would it? When I would rediscover the ability to go deep within myself? To unlock my creative zone? At my artistic best, my fingers had Harry Potter wands attached. Right now, at my worst, I was unable to pick up a brush.

The waitress went inside and Zen stepped toward me. "Well, lookie there."

Two cop cars and an ambulance pulled up in front of the bait house across from Bert's. Traffic was at a standstill. A crowd of onlookers watched as the officers left their cars and hurried toward the building. An ambulance approached. We moved toward the curious medley of peeps.

"Anyone know what's happening?" I shot a glance from one set of eyes to another.

A woman in white silk pants and a low-cut turquoise tank top pointed. "That guy called the cops. That's all I know."

Zen's and my head rotated at the same pace. Russ Beadle, a burly crabber we both knew, stood near two other rough-around-the-gills guys sipping from beer bottles. Zen and I raised our eyebrows at each other and weaved their way.

"What's up?" I stood shoulder to shoulder to Beadle.

He nodded at me, but his eyes remained riveted on the door.

"I heard what I thought was an engine backfirin`. Was goin` into Bert's for a beer, but something about the sound didn't set right with me, soz I trot across the road to make sure Stoner is okay. The door's locked. I look into the window and sees legs sticking out from behind the counter. His shoes and the copper-colored hair on his ankles showed me it weren't Stoner, so I called the cops." He looked at Zen. "You can bet if I thought it was Stoner I woulda broke through the damn door right then."

Zen nodded in a manner that said she totally understood. Anyone who knew Beadle was aware that he'd been in prison numerous times. Why would he want cops down his neck again?

"But then I figured the guy might still be alive, soz I kicks the door in. Poor sucker. Dead as a chunk of chum. Shot in the face from what I could tell—couldn't tell who it was. It weren't pretty."

The ambulance came to a get-out-of-my-way stop in front of the parked cars, trucks, and Harleys at Bert's and the bait shop. By this time, all of the parked vehicles had emptied out. The crowd had grown to the size of a popular movie premier audience. Words hissed through the air. A lone osprey stood watch from a telephone pole. A cell phone buzzed. And then another. Pungent human sweat and pithy perfume merged.

The paramedics hurried into the building and shortly after, with heads down, went to their ambulance, pulled out a portable gurney and carried it inside. Whispers became loud grumbles.

As Zen leaned toward me to speak, Tobin Peterson, with a bandaged head, came outside. He spoke to the closest person, a woman with blonde, broom-like hair. She pointed toward Beadle who downed his beer, handing the empty to the guy at his side.

"You the one who found the vic?" Tobin asked.

Zen and I took two steps back while Beadle related the same story he had just told us. Tobin said he would have to come down to the station and repeat his statement. Beadle agreed.

Tobin went to the cruiser and spoke to another officer, made a phone call, then turned, caught my eye and walked toward me and Zen.

Last season when Tobin had asked me out for that date I'd said no. Not because I hadn't thought he was cute and might be fun to go out with, but when he had asked, I was involved with Jay Mann and I'm a one man kind of woman.

"Jessie. Zen." Tobin's dark hair was clipped close to his head. His nose was long, ears small. His piercing eyes met mine. I yanked my tan cap lower, hoping it covered my reddened cheeks.

"I need you to come down to the station with me."

My eyebrows shot up. Zen, who never approved of Tobin for the mere reason that he was a man of the law and anyone knew *they* weren't to be trusted, took a protective step toward me.

Tobin straightened to his full height. His face went wooden. "This is official business. Please come with me."

Astonished by his officious tone, I glanced at Zen. She looked as surprised and perplexed as I did, but she found her voice first.

"What's this all about? Jessie just arrived. She can't…"

He twisted around and stopped her words with a stern, off-putting, overbearing gaze. My heart did a flip flop. The crowd began to mutter again. Many knew Zen. She was a permanent resident. Some most likely knew me. I'd gotten notoriety from both helping to solve two local crimes and from newspaper spreads about my art which was now hanging in the Matlacha Gallery and a gallery in Fort Myers. All around us, like flames on a newly lit gas stove, anger ignited. Zen took my arm.

Tobin raised his voice. "This is a murder investigation. We are taking Ms. Murphy in to ask her some questions—nothing more." He stepped aside. "Jessie?"

I was truly mystified. What did he think I could know about a shooting that had happened most likely before I had even arrived in Matlacha?

Assuring Zen I'd see her later that night, I followed him to his cruiser. As he opened the back door, the paramedics came outside pulling and pushing the gurney that now held a fully covered body. I slid onto the car seat. A loud "ahhh" came from the crowd as Tobin slammed the car door. The sound reminded me of the time I'd dropped the lid of an old chest of my grandma's. Metal had hit metal so fast that one of her favorite vases fell off a shelf and broke into a thousand pieces.

The sound of that cherished glass breaking echoed in my head.

4

The day had been a pisser; what with the long hours in the car, the near accident and strange behavior of the driver and passenger, the shooting, and now this.

Nearing Veterans Parkway the stop lights were misty splotches of diffused color as the signal changed from red to green. The brake lights of the ambulance glowed in the steamy, vaporous air, creating a gloomy radiance that caught my attention. The cross painted across the doors shimmered with an eerie glow as it turned right onto the Parkway.

Tobin drove in concentrated silence, glancing only occasionally at me through the windshield mirror while I remained puzzled and uninformed in the back seat.

Angry and frustrated to the max, I reached for my cell phone to text Hawk to ask for advice, but my pocket was empty. I'd left it to charge at the inn. All I had with me was a twenty dollar bill I'd stuffed into my jean's pocket for beer and a burger. No driver's license. No credit cards. I wasn't handcuffed, but I felt as if I were. It was an odd realization that stayed with me on the half-hour trip. All my attempts to ask Tobin questions fell on deaf ears. I concentrated on the passing cars.

At the sheriff's office where I'd been to on several occasions, the parking lot was near empty. Overhead, a continuous stream of sea gulls headed in the direction of the Gulf, flapping their wings, squawking an ominous red-flag sound. We had hardly reached the front door before a thin brisk woman in a police uniform met us.

The officer directed penetrating and questioning eyes on me, but merely stepped back to let us pass. I wanted to bolt, but where would I go?

Inside, Tobin led me down the terrazzo-floored hallway and into a small room that contained only a metal industrial table and three chairs. I'd watched enough cop shows to know it was an interrogation room. I wondered if someone watched me through the one-way glass that filled the upper wall to the right of the door. I focused on Tobin.

"What's this about? Why am I here? Why all the blasted silence?"

Giving a quick nod, he stepped out of the room and shut the door.

Just like that.

I released a captured whiff of air and reached for the door handle. This had to be illegal. They couldn't keep me here. But as I pulled the door toward me, Sheriff White walked into the room causing me to back-pedal.

"Ah, Miss Murphy. Nice to see you again," she said. "Just arrived?"

Her friendly expression and warm demeanor was a startling contrast to Tobin's treatment. Couple this with my frayed nerves and exhausted state, and the wild idea that had just popped into my head that I'd been kidnapped by some weird aliens who'd taken over the bodies of local cops, I blanched and sunk onto a chair. The fact I hadn't eaten lunch or dinner probably didn't help either.

The sheriff stepped out of the room and requested water be brought in while I stared blankly at the scratched table top.

The female cop I'd seen outside hurried in and plunked down a filled paper cup in front of me. I downed it in one gulp.

After that cop left, Sheriff White took the chair that faced me. I rubbed the back of my neck. "It's been a long day. Just why am I here?" I asked. "And why couldn't Tobin Peterson answer my questions?"

The sheriff smiled and folded her arms on the table. "He was following my orders. I apologize for your confusion. I knew he was, er is, attracted to you and I didn't want him influencing this investigation by giving you a sympathetic edge. In fact, I wanted another officer to bring you in, but under the circumstances—which I won't go into—that was impossible. I assure you Officer Peterson was as uncomfortable with his silence and treatment of you as you were by receiving it."

Her little speech didn't make me feel any less un-kidnapped, but I let it go. "So?"

"The vic had a photo of you on his cell phone."

I sat up straighter. My voice quivered like a violin string. "He knew me?"

"It appears so. I'd like to take you to the morgue, if you don't mind, to help us identify him as quickly as possible. He was carrying no driver's license. No identification whatsoever—only his cell phone. We're getting in contact with the owner of the shop, but your help would be appreciated. You won't be able to tell much from his face."

I bit my lip as she told me how there was very little left of that. As we headed for the morgue our footsteps echoed and all I could think about was being anywhere but there. The sheriff pushed open the door. The coroner stepped back from a table. We neared.

"Don't worry, I've covered the damaged area," the coroner assured me.

I relaxed—kind of.

He unveiled the upper half of the body with, yes, the face draped under a white cloth.

I gasped. My eyes widened. The carrot-red hair. The rooster comb.

In quick, short sentences I told the sheriff the story of the earlier episode on the highway. My gaze switched to the medical cabinet on the far wall. Everything was so sterile. So clean. So perfect. So orderly. Except this poor man in this dreadful place. My eyes teared up. "This guy had a photo of ME!?"

The sheriff nodded.

I laid the back of my hand over my mouth and looked back at the stout body. If this stranger had a photo of me, it must mean that he was my stalker. Why had he attempted to run me off the road? How long had he been following me? And who was the woman who had run?

It's the strangest thing to gaze at the lifeless face of a man who might have been obsessed with you and who had made your life a living hell. In death, he didn't look threatening. In fact, he looked innocent, so very ordinary that it was difficult for me to think badly of him. Yet I would never forget my terror as I had gone about my days realizing that someone might know where I was at any given time, that any sense of privacy or security was no longer a surety. How many times had I imagined myself shooting him or plunging a knife into his heart? And here he might be, no longer a threat.

After returning to the interrogation room, the sheriff showed me the photo and asked if she could record our conversation. I agreed. The photo had been taken last season at the gallery opening Luke Abbot had sponsored. I was standing in front of one of my oil paintings.

I spent the next hour filling in the sheriff about my experiences with the stalker. It had begun with phone calls—heavy breathing, no words. Gradually more aggressive actions included unsigned cards professing love in my mailbox, a love note placed on my nightstand, and flowers addressed to me showing up in various places.

I ended with: "The Cambridge cops had no luck catching him."

The sheriff switched off the tape recorder. The click gave me a start. I looked at the sheriff. Her expression was blank. "What time did you say you arrived in Matlacha?"

I blinked several times. Of course she'd ask this. I had just given her a perfect motive for murder.

"Around four. Zen was waiting for me. She can vouch for the time."

The sheriff's eyes locked with mine. "Is there any reason I should doubt your word?"

I shook my head. "No, of course not."

"That's what I thought. Well . . ." She stood. "You must be exhausted. Such a long trip. I'll have Officer Davis take you back to Matlacha. Officer Peterson will be tied up with paperwork."

5

It was 10:30 when we reached the Bridgewater Inn. Rain had stopped falling. A nonmenacing breeze blew from the west, and paler clouds drifted across the sky. A crescent moon peeped around the gray edges. It was clear enough that I could see for some distance and I made out a man on a sailboat moored in the Gulf.

The inn had been built on pilings that had recently been replaced. The entrance faced Pine Island Road.

I thanked the deputy and soon walked by the blue, yellow, and green Adirondack chairs fashioned into fish shapes wondering why they had seemed dull when I arrived just hours before. That I was tired was an understatement. A mullet jumped and slapped the water as I took the key out of my jean's pocket and began to slide it into the lock. But the door popped open first and Zen all but fell into my arms. Pulling me close, she pressed her head against my chest.

Taken aback—I mean I hadn't been gone *that* long—I moved her to arm's length. "Hey! What's up?"

Zen was shaking so much her teeth chattered. She'd been crying.

"Oh, Jessie!" She burst into tears and I led her to the chairs near the window. Collapsing onto one, she swiped the back of her hand across her nose.

I assumed I would hear a story about a boating accident. They were far too prevalent down here. Last week Zen had phoned me about a tragedy where one boat had run into another and a favorite college coach had been killed. Zen had taken it real hard.

Zen refused to look at me. I could tell she was trying to figure out how to tell me something, but what? My eyes roamed right to left, darted back to the nightstand. "Where's Gar?"

"Oh! That's what I . . . Oh, Jessie! He's gone! When I came to your door it was unlocked, I thought you beat me here so I barged right in. Oh, Jessie, I'm so sorry."

Frantic, I began to search the room, starting with the nightstand drawer. I was relieved to see my iPad. When I pulled out my black bag, the bulge of my secret weapon was still there. Praying the intruder had only moved Gar, I continued my search.

"I already searched. He ain't here," Zen said.

I was heartsick. Gar might only be made of plaster of Paris, but he was my bud and the closest connection I had with my murdered lover, Will Rollins.

I sank onto the bed. "Why would someone take Gar?"

My eyes locked with Zen's.

Although it was at least 80 degrees in the room, I shivered.

Zen phoned the cops and they assured her they would come as soon as they could. Not so much because Gar had been taken, but because someone had broken into my apartment. There'd been a robbery and shooting at a North Fort Myers convenience store and that took precedence over a break-in where nothing but a gargoyle statue had been stolen and no one was seriously hurt.

I warned Zen not to touch anything as the intruder may have left fingerprints.

"You think you should change rooms?"

"Let's see what the cops say."

The cops never showed. Zen, at my insistence, left at 1 a.m.

After adding the occurrence in my iPad, I climbed under the sheets and hugged a pillow to my chest. I tossed. I turned. I bit down on my lip. Slipped out of bed. Pulled out my bag. Opened it. Unzipped a compartment and withdrew the gun. My hand hovered over the box of bullets.

In truth, I wasn't a believer that to own a gun was a good idea. But in my line of business, Hawk finally convinced me that they were a necessary evil. There were too many guns out there in too many hands. Too many people were shot every day. If I was going to be hired to hunt down murderers, I had to face the fact they could be armed. Karate skills could only work if I was close. But, the gun, I reminded myself, was purchased for emergencies only. Be reasonable. The thieves could be a couple of goofy teenagers who drank too much and wanted to pull a prank. My stalker is dead. I am no longer in danger. Gar will show up.

I sighed. Hid the weapon again. Zipped up my bag and slid it under the bed.

I fell asleep to the sound of lapping water and the fear that whoever took Gar may have thrown him into Matlacha Pass, attempting to ignore the thought that I could be next.

6

The next morning, Zen arrived holding two cups of coffee as I finished tying my tennis shoes. "Cheer up," she said, handing me a paper cup, "We'll find him."

"Sure we will."

"Ah, come on, girl." Her tone was that of a teacher coaxing a kindergartner out of a storage closet. "I'll buy some notecards. You always use notecards to solve a crime, right?"

"I use my iPad now. But, listen up. I've been thinking."

I reviewed the series of events as Zen paced. For more than six months I'd been stalked. If the man at the morgue was my stalker and also the man at the earlier accident, how could he have arrived in Matlacha before me, broken into my room and stolen Gar?

"Does seem like he might be your stalker. Why else would he have your photo? But probably not the thief, right?"

"Yeah, I agree."

The efficiency seemed oppressively hot. I pushed myself to a standing position to open the window. Zen stopped her pacing and placed her hands on her broad hips. "Time to get busy?"

I nodded. Action, Grandma always advised, was the key to results. I wanted Gar back and I'd make it happen. Period.

Glancing at the empty spot where Gar should have been, I put on my lucky cap and retrieved my laughing cell phone from the nightstand.

"Hello."

"Jessie Murphy?"

"Yeah."

"This is the sheriff's office. There will be an officer there around 10."

That would give me plenty of time to powerwalk. Without my daily exercise my body or mind never fully awakened. This was also my best thinking and problem solving time. Zen and I headed outside. Zen, to her trailer for more coffee. Me, toward the community park to clear my head and get my day started right.

As I crossed the new bridge, I nodded at several fishermen: men, women, and kids with lines dangled over the rails, five-gallon buckets of bait, shrimp and pin fish near their feet. Some shrimp used for bait were bigger than the thumb of a large man. Usually I would stop to watch for dolphin, or to gab box with a friendly face, but Gar's loss and my need to completely shed my funk made me continue on at a rapid pace.

Traffic rolled by, causing the bridge floor to roar like a train. The American flag flapped in the breeze over the post office. The fudge shop "Open" sign was on. Good. They'd survived the off-season lull in business. I'd come to know and like one of the co-owners of the shop that had just opened last year. The other owner was a good guy too.

A horn honked. I startled. The driver waved. I raised my hand in greeting. Luke Abbot, the owner of the gallery in Matlacha was the who had first encouraged my painting and shown it. He slowed down, but a long line of cars and trucks nudged him forward.

I'd stop to see him later in the day. He knew my routine. Anyone who knew me more than a passing hello, realized how important these morning walks were for me. I continued on, raising my face to the welcoming sun. Thank God for sunscreen. I was a redhead with Irish blood. Without the lotion, I'd be one big freckle. Plus skin cancer was in the family. My mom had had three skin grafts on her legs. Phoenix, Arizona and ignoring warnings about the use of baby oil had been her downfall. Luckily Grandma hadn't been a sun worshiper and had spent most of her life in the Boston area inside her house.

I took a left, passing the Art Association building. A path encircled the park and its public boat ramp, kayak slide, tiny pebbled opening that really wasn't a beach by anyone's standards, shaded picnic benches, and fishing pier. Osprey, cranes, pelicans, egrets—all made it a stopping place.

I sat at a picnic table and stared into the dark water as I thought of Matlacha and what images I might use if I painted a scene today. If, that is, I could only paint, which I still couldn't: Sidewalk-less, narrow street. Mannequin—legs crossed—on rooftop gripping a heart-shaped sign heralding "Matlacha Spoken Here." Bling-studded bicycle trapped under an eve. Lawn controlled by more weed than grass. Skiff threatening to sink by the weight of crab traps. Kayaks slicing the water's surface. A coin-operated merry-go-round horse arrested on a heavy stabilized spring that kids rode for free. Matlacha—a place where revealed secrets sliced as deep and plentiful as fishing knives.

I stood, raised my arms and walked fast. Nothing I'd ever done that was important to me had been easy. I stopped to catch my breath. Nothing.

A pelican (Will's totem) swooped across the surface of the pass and landed on a piling. These birds with their wise eyes—so otherworldly, so god-like, so prehistoric—appeared at the darnedest times. I lowered my voice as if to pray and addressed it, "I've never had anything handed to me on a silver platter, have I?"

Or maybe I had and I just wasn't comfortable with it. Will, after all, had been more than generous. "You're killing me with your kindness," I used to say to him.

But he never got that. Couldn't get it.

I couldn't take my eyes off the bird. "Is this one thing too much to ask? This return of Gar?"

The bird spread its wings and shot high into the sky, then switched course and nose-dived. Its beak and head disappeared. When it resurfaced, a foot-long fish extended from its beak. The pelican flipped its head and changed the direction of its prey. Opening its mouth, the fish went down its throat. Just like that. Nature's way. One loss of life. One sustained life. Another adult that knew it had to feed herself before she could help others. As it wasn't, but now always would be. *Get to work, Jessie. Get to work.* Grandma Murphy's words were as loud as the slap of the pelican's wings on the water. "Amen," I whispered.

Exhaling, raising my arms, I moved on, ready to start my search. All that I could do at this point was to ask questions of the inn manager and residents as to whether they'd seen a shady character last night. Then see where that took me. I hesitated and hunkered down, plucking a pebble from the path. It was oval, dark gray and had a ring of lighter color encircling it. A lucky stone. I smiled, lifted my head and said "Thank you" before I dropped it into my pocket.

By the time I got back to the inn, sweat dripped down my forehead and under my arms. I rounded the building and ran into Tobin Peterson. He wasn't in uniform and his jeans fit like a Speedo. His shirt was long-sleeved, buttoned at the wrists. My first thought—had they found Gar?

31

"Don't you normally run earlier than this?"

"Usually." I looked at him out of the corner of my eye. Despite the sheriff's explanation, I was still angry at him for his treatment of me at the murder scene and after. Forgiveness wasn't my best suit.

"Ah, come on. Give me a break. The sheriff wouldn't let me say anything. I was under strict orders. Can't we have coffee or something?"

Hmm . . .

"Maybe I could help you," he added, giving me a puppy-dog look.

Well . . .

His more than sincere eyes were the same green as a palm frond. I'm a sucker for green or blue or brown, for that matter. The leaves in the tree over his head swayed. Clusters of pink bougainvillea blossoms created a frame around his tanned, Romanesque face. Well . . .

And just like that, I caved in like a roll of rice paper stepped on by a Suma wrestler.

Knowing I smelled like a four-day-old dead fish washed up on a beach, I suggested we meet at the Perfect Cup for breakfast after my shower. He took the hint and said he'd meet me there.

Okay, okay. It's true. I liked the idea of getting assistance from an off-duty cop, especially one with six-pack abs. Call me shallow, but, well . . . just call me shallow. I took my time in the shower. Lathered every part of my body. Rinsed thoroughly. Towel dried my hair and pulled it back into a ponytail. I'm fortunate to have a thick mane, but drying it is a bear. I donned a tan T-shirt, shorts, flip flops and my lucky tan cap.

32

The Perfect Cup was across the bridge on the other side of the road next to CW Fudge Factory. Tobin sat at a table for two near the entrance on the right. I nodded at him. He rose and we went to the back for coffee. Waitresses served the tables, but coffee was self-serve. It wasn't high season—that began after New Year's, but the place was full.

We chatted about nothing as we carried our cups to the table. Several people smiled at me and I nodded at them.

Tobin immediately asked me to relate what had happened from my interview with the sheriff to what happened at the inn, leaving nothing out. He listened intently while I talked.

"Anything else missing?"

"Nope. Just my bud."

Tobin drained his cup. The waitress came, took our order and left.

"Odd thing to take." He leaned forward on his arms.

I pushed back against my chair.

"Yeah, very odd. It's not like he's valuable or anything. I mean, I rescued him from being picked up by a garbage truck."

"And the guy in the morgue had a photo of you on his phone?"

"Yeah. I have to assume he was the one stalking me."

"Stalking you?"

He didn't know about my stalker? REALLY?

The waitress arrived with the food. Tobin excused himself to refill our mugs while I arranged the details of my stalking story in my head. Tobin returned and while we ate I gave him the facts, leaving out the detail that Tobin was on my list of possible stalkers. At one point in my story, Tobin became angry, later he seemed downright sad.

33

I ended with, "For a split second I thought my stalker stole Gar. Like for an odd love token or something. But the guy who was murdered had my picture. Why would a stranger have my picture? He had to be my stalker. And I can't imagine that guy having time to arrive in Matlacha before me, steal Gar and then get murdered."

"Jessie, I can't believe you didn't tell me that someone was stalking you. You know I would have helped. It's not like we didn't have each other's phone numbers."

"Ah, I just figured I could take care of myself. I never felt really threatened, but scared? Oh, yeah. I was scared all right. I felt so blasted vulnerable." Feeling a tad bit unsettled, I glanced at the wall clock: 9:30. The on-duty cops were coming at 10. "Listen, I need to go."

"I'm offering my services. If there's anything I can do, let me know."

"Thanks, I appreciate that."

"You have a plan?"

I pursed my lips. "Just to question the manager and other inn guests. Nothing earth shattering."

"Why don't we talk again tonight at dinner?" he asked.

"Okay."

Jessie, you didn't even hesitate. That was the voice of my grandma speaking in my head. I resisted rolling my eyes.

We agreed he would pick me up at 7:30. He insisted upon paying for the coffee and food, but I shook my head and reached into my pocket. As I pulled out the money, the pebble I'd found on my walk came out too. I closed my fist around it and dropped it back into my shirt, then plonked three dollar bills on the table. Tobin grimaced and shoved the money back at me.

"Put that away, I'm paying."

I lowered my eyes. A man whose ego couldn't let a woman pay her portion of a bill in public? Really?

A stocky man with a Mohawk walked toward me. I stiffened. Relaxed when he passed. Sliding the money to the center of the table, I gave Tobin my attention. "Any chance the sheriff knows the name of the murder victim?"

"Actually, I think she does."

"Think she'd share the info with me?"

"It'll be public information soon. But I'll be happy to get it for you."

I touched my hat and opened the door. When I stepped back to let in two women, I noticed that Tobin had a scowl on his face as he folded the money into his pocket.

I smiled.

7

The two cops who came to my room were pleasant enough and seemed to listen intently to my account of the break-in and theft. I gave Zen's name to the shorter, stockier one who held a pad and pen.

The second man with graying hair had gone back to the door and was inspecting it.

"The door wasn't locked?"

"Uh, no." Not locking doors was a bad habit I thought I'd broken since being stalked, but apparently in my hurry to go out with Zen I'd reverted to my former lax ways.

The cop straightened to his full height. "I'd say you're lucky nothing else was stolen. Those paint supplies and that iPad look like they'd bring a pretty penny at a pawn shop. What would you say is the, uh, gargoyle's monetary worth?"

"Invaluable."

"I see. Well, I'd say the thief was surprised by your friend and grabbed the nearest item before scramming. What was the item made of?'

"Plaster of Paris."

"Any inlaid jewels? Diamonds? Emeralds? Pearls?"

I puckered my lips and shook my head. "Nah, I found him at a garbage can."

His lips played with a smile. "I see, unfortunately, the item, uh, I suspect . . . is actually only worth a few bucks at best."

Normally I would have to control my urge to give the insensitive guy a karate chop. Instead I merely sniffed (but loudly, I assure you). Gar was the one object I had that Will, the love of my life, and I had owned together. When Gar was close, Will was close. To say that Gar was almost worthless was like saying love meant nothing.

The jerk pocketed the pad and pen and looked at his partner. "You agree, Jake?"

"Yeah. I'd say it was someone out for some quick money who was going around the inn checking doors. The thing just might show up at a garage sale." He looked at me. "Your door at the inn is apparently the only one that happened to be unlocked." He didn't call me a fool out loud, but I saw it in his eyes.

After suggesting I secure my doors in the future, the men left. I sat in the easy chair and stared at the flat surface on the nightstand where Gar was supposed to be.

I picked up my iPad and opened a folder, labeling it "Gar Gone Missing." My tasks were simple:

1. Talk to the manager and other guests to see if they saw or heard anything out of the ordinary last night.

2. Check consignment stores and garage sales on Pine Island and along Pine Island Road.

3. Call the sheriff and find out the name of the murdered man. Although doubtful, somehow the incidents might be connected.

I thought for several moments, but came up with no number four.

Avoiding looking at the empty nightstand surface, I put the iPad in my red child-sized backpack and slid my arms through the straps. Cap in hand, I left the room, heading for the office.

The woman behind the counter had jet black hair and gorgeous dark olive skin. When I asked if she'd seen or heard anything suspicious last night, she didn't hide her irritation.

"Did you have the statue insured? We don't carry insurance for personal belongings."

I told her that Gar's value had nothing to do with a price tag and admitted to leaving the door unlocked. Her relief was obvious and she said she'd seen or heard nothing. I left shortly after and knocked on every door with no result.

Disappointed, I headed for the Matlacha Gallery. Luke Abbot, the owner, was a man with a sunny disposition who knew that Gar was more than a mere object to me. I was normally an upbeat gal, but the stalking thing and now Gar's theft had taken a lot out of me. I had hoped that coming to Matlacha would give me back my sparkle.

I hesitated as I stood looking up at the side of the building. The wall-sized pelican I'd painted two seasons ago to honor Will was beginning to fade. One of these seasons I needed to touch it up. I ducked my head and went to the front.

The door to Luke's truck bed was open. Luke was in the main gallery setting a box on the floor. When he saw me, he rushed over and we hugged. As I expected, he'd already heard about the murder and the theft. News travels like a jagged bolt of lightning in Matlacha. His hug tightened. Luke was one of those sincere types. When he said he was sorry that Gar had been stolen, I knew he meant it.

We went out back and sat at a cement table covered in colorful broken tiles near a faded green and purple gazebo. Bougainvilleas were in full bloom, but laden with dust. A blue wine-bottle tree seemed lackluster and in need of polishing. Small Disney plastic figures that had been pressed into a cement ledge lined a pathway leading to a narrow canal.

I related the recent events of my life as a black cormorant landed on the edge of a wooden boat filled with coconuts. Straightening itself, it spread its wings, blocking my view of the canal.

"Stalked? You've been being stalked and didn't tell me? Oh, Jessie."

It was embarrassing to admit that Luke, like Tobin, was on my list of possible stalkers. The fact was, any man I had ever met and who I thought was at all interested in me in the slightest, was on the list. That's how crazed being stalked had made me.

I suppressed my urge to not tell him this information and confessed.

Luke was silent for so long I was afraid I had offended him more than our friendship could bear.

But to my relief, Luke took both my hands in his. "You know what you need to do?"

"What?"

"Why don't you sketch a picture of Gar and make posters, then hang them up all over the island, Pine Island too? That way everyone, tourists and all, would know he was stolen and will be on the lookout for him."

I gnawed on my lower lip. I hadn't been able to draw or paint for so long I wasn't sure I could anymore. I'd brought my supplies in hopes, but . . .

"Oh, Jessie! Don't tell me that you're not painting again?"

Gazing at my toes, I nodded. Luke knew my art had for years taken a back seat while I worked too many long hours as an apartment manager in Boston. My urge to create again had only resurfaced on a regular basis the winter I came back to find out what had really happened concerning Will's death.

Luke spent the next five minutes lecturing me about how important it was for an artist to create. When he was finished I promised him I would try. But I wasn't convinced I had it in me. Over the last months, the more I felt watched, the less I created.

But dutifully, sullenly, not expecting much, I returned to my room and picked up my sketchpad and pencil, sat outside on the dock and doodled. Scribbles at first. Lines that meant nothing. Circles that went nowhere. Stars that didn't twinkle. Boxes that didn't open. In the end, it was my overpowering desire to get Gar back that broke through the thick brick wall of my mind. Gar's pointed ears, and his ugly but cute face appeared on the page.

When the pencil sketch was finished, I drove to the printing company on Pine Island with the drawing and the guy there helped me make a poster. I made twenty copies and stopped in every business establishment and the library to hang them. No one refused. Everyone was sympathetic. No one had seen Gar swooping the shore.

I was done by 6:30, an hour before Tobin was to arrive. Luke and Grandma were right. I did feel better after taking action. Not 100 percent but better. While inquiries at the inn had led to nothing, the sketches could maybe get better results. Plus, I felt a slight hint of hope that I would be able to paint again. It had been too long.

I showered. Dropped a lavender flowered dress over my head. Smoothed out the skirt. Stepped into black flip flops. Stood in front of the bathroom mirror with my red mane in one hand. Pulled it behind my head. Clasped it with a turquoise clip. Grimaced. Leaned closer to my reflection. My dark circles didn't seem as prominent. Not quite anyway. I stuck out my tongue and touched the tip of my nose.

Knock. Knock. Knock.

I straightened my shoulders and went to the door.

Tobin was dressed in jeans and a tan T-shirt. Those hard-to-resist baby greens met mine. I looked away.

Despite my glum mood, our meal had a joyous tone. It seemed Tobin's mission was to cheer me up. I had never seen him so animated. He spoke of many subjects—on the state of art in Florida, on the plays being performed at the Lab Theatre in Fort Myers, on Morgan guitars, on underground, spiritual ley lines, and on the future of humor. Intermittent jokes added to this new "Tobin." I was amazed and impressed. While he talked I found my dusty mood taking a back seat. Neither of us alluded during our lobster dinner to Gar or to the murder victim.

When the plates were cleared, Tobin glanced at me almost shyly and refilled our wine glasses.

He raised his glass. "To a new us."

I hesitated, then lifted my glass as well. "To a *slow* new us," I said.

His grin faltered briefly, but returned.

We were the last folks to leave. The parking lot was almost empty.

"Beautiful night." Tobin slipped my arm through his and I let him. He steered me toward the back of the restaurant.

And I let him.

Moonlight lit the pilings painted like totem poles. Mangrove leaves gleamed more silver than deep green. Water caressed the seawall as we settled on a bench. The smell of pungent sea life mixed with the cuk cuk cuk of an osprey reminded me that I was a lucky woman to be able to be here. Not all people my age could winter in Florida while maintaining a life up north. But I worked hard for this.

Figuring out what kind of life I wanted after I'd lost Will had taken me some time and I'd spent many hours worrying over the decision. Once the decision had been made, I determined how to make it happen. Not that my life was ideal—far from that.

A cloud mountain drifted over and blocked the moon. Looked like a storm was imminent. The closeness of Tobin's body brought back a dim memory of my dad. He had died when I was four and I had few stored pictures of him in my mind, but suddenly he was there beside me comforting me after I had fallen off my three-wheeled bike and skinned my knee. Red hair unkempt. Green eyes concerned.

Tobin pulled me closer and talked about his last vacation. Hiking, tent camping, catch and release fishing. His voice was low, soothing, and musical. Could I really be attracted to this traditionally minded man? Will had been a free spirit. A man who defied institutional living. Jay Mann, my brief fling last season, was a sculptor, a loner, certainly not a team player like a cop had to be.

Just as I was beginning to feel smothered, a twig snapped behind us. Startled, I looked over my shoulder. Tobin exclaimed and jumped up as a figure dressed in a head to ankle yellow rain slicker holding what looked like a gun disappeared around the corner.

Tobin took chase first. I followed, but the man ran like a deer, leaping and zigzagging. I raised my arms and pumped. My stride lengthened and I caught up with Tobin. Just a few more yards and we'd be able to touch the flapping slicker and yank him to the ground. I could smell his fear, or was that my own?

With one more step, Tobin tripped, grunted, and went down. I hesitated. "Get him," he growled. I took up the chase again, my heart, a drummer gone mad.

One more stride and . . .

Making a sound like a native Calusa war call, the guy leapt over the seawall and landed with a loud thud.

As I came to a sliding, abrupt halt, an engine started up and in the next instant a boat shot into the pass. The moon remained behind the clouds. The phantom sea craft was more mirage than entity. If it weren't for the roar of the engine, because of the shadow the boat made, it would have been easy to imagine it was a sea creature hightailing it for a distant island.

Gasping for breath, I bent over, inhaled deeply and caught my breath. Powerwalking was a natural for me. Running? Not so much.

Straightening, I returned to Tobin's side. He was struggling to stand on one foot.

"Got away?"

"Afraid so."

8

The next morning I was awakened by my phone. It was the sheriff. She was on the way to see me and would arrive in about twenty minutes. I clicked off and saw it was 8:30. I normally don't sleep that late. Apparently the excitement of last night and the fact I hadn't fallen to sleep until around 3 a.m. had taken its toll. I stood and stumbled to the bathroom and then made a pot of coffee. No one wants to see or talk to me before a cup of coffee. No one.

I had just finished brushing my hair when someone knocked. I hurried over and pulled open the door. The blast of sunlight made me cringe.

"Special delivery," a voice behind a large bouquet of zinnias and baby breath said. A face lit up by grin appeared and he thrust the flowers at me. My eyes widened. He left so quickly I didn't have time to thank or to tip him.

Wide-eyed, I stared at the flowers for the longest time.

They're from Tobin. They are.

Holding the flowers at arm's length I carried them to the sink and leaned them against its side while I looked for something I could use for a vase. With a quivering hand, I settled for a quart Ball jar someone had left in a cupboard.

They're from Tobin. I know they are.

I arranged them in the jar and placed them on the table under the window.

They're from Tobin, I assured myself again.

If you are so sure, why aren't you opening the card? I bit down on my lip. My eyes watered. I shot a look at the nightstand.

Someone knocked again. Not knowing why I did it, I quickly set the bouquet on the floor near the side of the bed where it couldn't easily be seen. Clearing my throat, I walked across the room and opened the door.

Sheriff White's face was solemn as she entered. I offered her a cup of coffee, but she refused. I refilled my mug. My gaze remained glued to her face as I sat on one of the chairs motioning for her to take the other. Reaching to my right, I pulled on the cord of the window shade. The light streaming in the window illuminated the multi-colored blonde strands of the sheriff's hair. But "having a blonde moment" she wasn't exuding.

"I'm sorry to bother you so early in the morning, but I have to meet someone in Pine Island, so thought I'd stop by. I understand you and Officer Peterson were accosted last night."

"Well, not exactly. But the person did have a gun." I took another sip of java.

"So I understand from the report. Were you sure it was a revolver?"

I hesitated. "Actually . . . well . . . no."

"It could have been some other shiny object that appeared to be a gun?"

"Well . . . perhaps."

The sheriff shuffled in her chair. "From the report I read, it appears someone walked up behind you and Officer Peterson and startled you. You thought they had a gun and took chase. Is this right?"

"Yes."

The flowers are from Tobin. Surely, they are.

"We had a tourist come in this morning and report an incident where he was chased by a man and woman last night near the Sandy Hook in Matlacha."

I frowned. "A tourist?"

"Yes, it appears he had taken his flashlight into the restaurant to help him get back to his boat and as he was leaving to follow the path back to where he had tied up, two crazy people chased him."

"Whoa! Really? A tourist?"

"Yes, Ms. Murphy, an innocent tourist. His description of the two assailants was very specific. I convinced him to not file charges, but I do suggest you be more careful in the future. We know you are stressed out because of your past experience with a stalker, but we don't want to frighten our bread and butter, do we?"

"But Tobin . . ."

"Officer Peterson assures me that he has been concerned about your state of mind. He is aware that he can be over-protective where females are concerned. He thinks it is quite possible that he overreacted."

I'm sure my face was the color of a pickled beet. I couldn't imagine the ribbing that Tobin was taking. To have sprained his ankle chasing a tourist. Oh, no. I almost laughed out loud.

I nodded and followed her out to the dock. As she rounded the corner, a man strolled toward me, Jolly Christopher from the candy shop. I was the only one who added the "Jolly" to his name and he always chuckled when I did.

"Oh, honey, what's going on here? I've been watching the sheriff's car forever and I just couldn't wait any longer. You poor thing. Do tell."

46

I couldn't help but laugh. I pulled Christopher into the room and shut the door.

As an owner of the local candy shop, Jolly Christopher had lots of people coming into the store telling him humorous anecdotes and staying longer than necessary to brighten their day. It was the foundation of his business, the brick and mortar—sweetness and light. I needed some sweet light right now. He sat. I picked up the vase of flowers and placed them on the table.

Smiling at the bouquet, Christopher threw his arm over the back of the chair, crossed his legs and began to talk. The tiny mole under his right eye crinkled as he spoke. "'So, Gator said, "my goal is to catch the biggest catfish in the area.'"

I refused to look at the flowers.

Christopher continued: "So I say, Catfish? In Matlacha? Is that PC? Aren't our fish more exotic than that? And Gator says, 'I don't give a fig if it's PC. Do ya think I care about PC? I want my mug in the paper holdin` that bugger. And I just might want a plaque too.'"

I chuckled and shook my head. Leave it to Gator. This was tarpon and deep sea fishing water—a place where giant fish leapt into the air several times before being hauled in. Tourists didn't come here for bottom-feeder catfish. Tourists wanted bragging rights.

"No one," I said, grinning, "brags about catching catfish down here."

Christopher's eyes twinkled. "Except Gator." He ran his fingers through his swept back longish chestnut hair. His white gold cat's eye ring caught in a curl at the nape of his head and he very carefully and gently untangled it. His movements were like those of a man who knew he had looks women admired. His presentation of a humorous anecdote

47

was stand-up comedian. Thinking of Gator on the front page of *The Eagle* showing off a catfish made me laugh like a kid at a birthday party until I was afraid I would pee my pants. Christopher joined in.

Then, wiping tears from his eyes, Christopher bent forward. "Honey, those are just some of the mostest bea…u…ti…ful zinnias I've ever seen. Do you know where they come from? Maybe I should think of carrying flowers in my shop."

I straightened my shoulders and pulled the card out of the bouquet. "Tobin Peterson sent them, I'm sure. He's the flower giving type. You'll have to ask him."

"Tobin Peterson? Do tell," he said with a chuckle.

"Tah, tah, tah, tah…" I sang as I extracted the card from its envelope, read the words and then closed my eyes to stop the tears from falling.

"Oh, honey. What!?"

I looked at Christopher and read aloud slowly, pronouncing each word with care: "From your loving soulmate. So happy your trip was uneventful."

I crumbled the card in my hand. I felt sick to my stomach, lightheaded. I started to stand, but feeling weak and unsteady, sat down again. Christopher insisted that I call the sheriff. I just wanted to call my grandma, but knowing she wouldn't answer the phone, in the end, decided he was right. The sheriff said we would have to come to the station.

By the time we arrived, I had my emotions under control. Christopher hardly said a word as he drove.

The sheriff, who luckily was in her office, told me to come in while Christopher remained in the waiting area.

I was surprised when she said she had been getting ready to phone me. We sat and she read the card, then slid it into a plastic bag. She cleared her throat and assured me that technicians would check for fingerprints and compare the handwriting to other notes I had received in the past year. Apparently they'd already been ordered from the Cambridge police, which was another jolt. There was no doubt as far as I was concerned that the bouquet was from the same person.

The sheriff leaned forward on her arms. "We located your gargoyle."

I jettisoned out of my seat, startling the sheriff who half stood.

"You found him? Wonderful! Where is he?"

"Please, Ms. Murphy, sit down."

I lowered myself into the chair.

"We have to keep him as evidence."

"Evidence? For what?"

"There was a robbery and the attendant was injured. He's in the hospital with a concussion."

I gazed at her in wonder.

"Your gargoyle, at least we believe it's yours, Officer Tobin provided us with a poster that seems to identify it as such, was found at the scene of the robbery."

"Gar!"

"The attendant at Quick Trip put up quite a struggle. The gargoyle, the wallet of the bait shop murder victim, and several photos of you were found in a canvas bag the assailant carried into the store."

My eyes, I was sure, were the size of key limes.

"Did you happen to have photos of yourself in your room that could have been stolen?"

I shook my head. "Not that I know of."

"Curious, isn't it? This is the second place where a crime was committed where photos of you were found."

I was stunned. "Surely the worker was able to identify the robber."

"The person wore a hoody and a ghost mask."

"But what about Gar? Was he hurt?"

"He appears to be intact. You can identify it before you leave. Once the investigation is over you'll be free to take it."

"And you think this has no connection with what happened last night?"

"We checked that possibility out, of course. But the tourist's alibi is sound. When he got back to his mooring, he went to other boaters anchored nearby and had a drink with them, relating his ordeal. They encouraged him to phone us last night, but he opted to wait for morning. He was at the office when I arrived. This is his sixth season of coming to Matlacha to fish. He is married with four grown kids. He is not your stalker and he did not have a gun in his hand last night when he startled you. As I said, it was a silver flashlight."

"And the murder victim at the bait shop?"

"That indeed was the driver of the van transporting pot who forced you off the road. But he was apparently also an old high school classmate of the bait shop owner, Steve (Stoner) Taylor. The dead man's name is Jonah Henning, but his nickname was apparently Rooster."

I couldn't help but picture his weird hairdo.

The sheriff continued. "He arrived a few hours earlier and Taylor was planning to run him home, but he had paperwork to finish up first. Taylor said he soon tired of his friend's excessive yammering about how he was missing his strawberry pie so he sent him to the shop to check on the shrimp tank. Less than an hour later he was killed."

50

"But why would someone I don't know who isn't my stalker have a picture of me?"

"Taylor apparently gave him your photo."

"Taylor?"

"Claimed he knew you were single and thought you and Henning might be a good match. Said he thought Henning should move on from taking care of his ex."

I blanched. A Matlacha dating service? Did the sheriff really buy this? Really? And why did Taylor have a photo of me?

"Was the bait shop incident a robbery attempt?"

"Could have been. There's been a lot of robberies in Lee County lately. Sign of the economy. Taylor said the cash register was full, but was untouched. Henning could have just been at the wrong place at the wrong time. Until we catch the murderer we won't know for sure."

"No fingerprints?"

"Oh, there were plenty. It's a bait shop. We're checking them out."

Neither of us spoke for several minutes.

"Ms. Murphy, about your stalker. In case you don't know, the average stalker is typically an unmarried white male. About a third of them are spouses or ex-lovers, a third are acquaintances, and a third strangers. They are often anti-social and loners. It is possible you will never know who he is."

"Yes, I know. I did my research."

"Are you connected to the popular social networks online?"

"Facebook. Twitter."

"It's possible for a loner to connect this way. Do make sure all your security boxes are checked."

Again, already warned.

"You do know that the majority of stalkers are not violent or threatening to those they stalk? Many finally give up and fade away."

Translation: Deal with it. Our officers are overworked. Chasing down stalkers is low on their "to do" list.

I left the office feeling down. Many stalkers never give up. Some kill those they stalk. But the Cambridge cops had said almost the same thing as the sheriff. I could only hope that the stalker developed another passion, and hopefully not a human one—something like watching old Laurel and Hardy movies or playing solitaire.

Gar was fine and apparently unharmed. That was a relief. But my stalker was still very much alive. What was it about me that attracted such types? Why couldn't I just have the garden variety boyfriend? Oh, no, not Jessie Murphy. She always had to be different.

Sometimes I envied all of my cousins. According to Grandma Murphy, they didn't have an ounce of magnetism surrounding them. They were bank tellers, garbage collectors, and insurance agents. They lived their lives covered by health insurance and when they retired would have pensions. None of them had ever had a stalker. You've got the allure curse, Grandma told me when I was five. You will always draw extremes to you.

Great. Just great. Could Grandma be wrong just once?

In the lobby, Christopher jumped up immediately wanting to know what happened. I gave him the lowdown. I could tell he was barely able to disguise a solemn expression, but somehow he did and managed to switch the conversation to his newest idea for a candy creation: Jessie Murphy Peanut Butter Fudge. Of course I chuckled.

It was November 28th. I'd been in Matlacha three days. It felt like a month.

After reconfirming that the statue was Gar and giving him a once over again, I hugged him and we left the building.

Putting his Chevy in reverse, Christopher missed hitting a fire hydrant by less than an inch, but he didn't miss a beat with his sweet talk. "I think I'll top the fudge with slivers of lime rind. Don't you think that's a great idea? Sweet and sour. Ah, so delectable. The customers will love it."

9

At exactly 8 p.m. (according to my phone) my eyes popped open from a nap I hadn't planned. What had awakened me? Voices? Sound of shoes hitting planks? No. A heavy knuckle knock. A loud one. I slid off the bed fully dressed and walked across the room. "Yeah, who's there?"

"It's me, woman, open up."

Russ Beadle? Yep, all two hundred and seventy-five tattooed, overall-adorned pounds of him. Yuck. My mind felt like it was still wrapped in a cotton sock of bad dream.

"What do you want? I'm not opening my door." I mumbled and ran my fingers through my tangled hair. Like I wanted this bruiser in my room?

Like, NOT!

"I have someone with me who wants to talk to you. Come on, open up. We won't bite."

I turned the knob, and leaving on the chain lock, opened the door a crack.

Beadle's forehead was crinkled. His lips slightly curled. "You were sleepin'?"

Beadle thought I was a sexless, boring nerd. The last time he'd come to my door I'd been in bed. If I remembered right it had been before 10 too. Whatever. Russ was the last person in Matlacha I wanted to impress by pretending cool. I yawned. Said nothing.

Another man stepped into my view. I couldn't place him. My guess was that he was in his late sixties, early seventies.

"This is Stoner Taylor. He wants to talk to you."

Ah, the Matlacha dating service guy? Great.

I nodded at him.

"Can we come in?"

Oh, sure you can. Absolutely.

I frowned and shot the lock, then opened the door and took a step their way. They backed up. I closed the door behind me and leaned against it casual-like, folding my arms. "What can I do for you?"

Beadle took two more steps back and stopped at the dock rail. Stoner, who was two heads shorter than Russ and one head shorter than me, had to look up to talk. Usually when I'm around men who are shorter than me I try to sit when we're close, but not this time. Stoner had passed around my picture. Hard telling what he said about me. Also, who knew where he got the photo?

"I need your help." His voice was squeaky and weak like a bird's first sound. This guy had to have had a tough childhood. His peers must have had a heyday with him. Short *and* cursed by a cartoon mouse's voice. Tough break. I walked to an Adirondack chair and sat. Stoner took the one facing me.

"My help?"

He knows you're a PI," Beadle said.

"I am *not* a PI."

"Yeah, sure."

I glared at Beadle. He shrugged and spit a wad of tobacco into the pass. A mullet jumped and slapped the water. I turned my shoulder to Beadle and looked at Stoner. Somewhere back in my brain a headache wiggled like an earthworm. "If he told you I'm a PI, he's mistaken."

"It wasn't him. I know who you are."

Dang that small town communication system. I pressed my lips together and glanced up at Venus. "All right. All right.

It's a bad time for me, but go ahead and tell me what you want."

Knowing that my stalker was alive and well didn't make me the best candidate for having all my rational faculties working efficiently. I wasn't going to share information with these two guys, especially with *these* two locals. Grandma's voice drifted through my mind: His friend was murdered. Remember?

Guilt. Big time. Thanks, Grandma. "Listen, I was rude. Sorry for your loss. I heard the man killed in your shop was a friend. That has to be tough."

I was taken aback when I saw his eyes tear. Sensitive dude too. Poor guy.

"He was more than a friend. He was my *best* friend." His hands shook as he accepted the discolored rag Beadle offered him. He blew his nose. I looked away. It was tough to see raw sorrow. I would never get used to it. I hoped.

"Rooster was a special guy. He had two kids to support and an ex-wife who had a stroke three years ago. He was doin' the best he could. The school district where he worked cut their budget and he was let go. And the worst of it is, I don't know why, but he was scared. Real scared."

I gnawed on my lower lip. He was getting to me and I didn't like it. "I was told by the cops that he had a photo of me on his cell phone."

"Yeah, I sent him that. When he asked if I knew anyone who could help him, I mentioned you. Zen said you were on the way down. He was on the way too. I figured if he had your photo and he ran into you before he and I met up, he could approach you."

"When did you take the photo?"

His face reddened. "At the end of last season. You were in Bert's. Sorry, I couldn't resist. My wife had just given me an iPhone. I went picture happy with it."

"So you weren't trying to set me up with a date?"

A smile came and went quickly from Stoner's face. "That's what I told the cops. Lame, isn't it? You and Rooster. Funny."

Beadle shifted his white boots. I refused to look at him.

"You didn't know why he was afraid?"

"He wouldn't tell me. Was even scared someone was buggin` his phone. I told him I didn't think anyone could do that on a cell, but he wasn't convinced. He was real paranoid. Wouldn't text me either."

"Did you tell this to the cops?"

"Nah, no use."

"Why?"

"They knew he had abandoned a van full of Colorado pot earlier in the day. They'd already tagged him for a criminal."

I kept what I knew to myself. "Telling them might help them find his murderer."

"I guess I'd like *you* to do that. Cops don't have much interest in finding drug smugglers' killers. I figure they're happy that one more is out of commission. Anyways, that's the impression I got from that woman sheriff."

Yes, I could see where he might get this idea. The sheriff didn't show much interest in finding my stalker either. I wondered if Stoner and I were millionaire tourists or locals the situation would be the same.

"Rooster would never have gotten involved with hauling drugs if it weren't for his family situation."

I knew Stoner was waiting for my reply. But was I up for this?

57

Stoner leaned forward. The look in his eyes was pure puppy-dog.

Dang.

"Will you help find his killer?"

I gazed out over the Gulf. A criminology course I'd taken with Hawk last fall had taught me a lot. This would be my first opportunity to use it. But . . . I . . .

Once again, Grandma came to my rescue: You can do this, Jessie. Forget what your mom said. Just be Jessie.

I straightened my shoulders and looked Stoner straight in the eye.

"Okay," I said in a firm voice, "if I'm to do this, it has to be done right. I charge fifty dollars an hour. I will need an assistant who will charge twenty dollars an hour. I charge mileage and I will need a retainer of $1,000. If the case is solved before the $1,000 is used up, you'll get a refund."

Whew!

"Well?"

Relief showed in his face. "I'll drop the retainer by in the morning." He looked from Beadle to me. "Unless you want it now, that is. I could run home and . . ."

"Tomorrow will be fine. That'll give me time to make up a contract to email you. You do have email?"

He nodded.

"Besides," Beadle said, "this woman goes to bed early."

I glared at him. "I'll email an itemized list of work completed once a week. Good?"

Stoner scratched his head in what looked like an act of agreement. We stood and shook hands. He jotted down his email address, and avoiding Beadle's eyes I turned to my door.

"Sleep tight," Beadle said before they started down the dock.

I gave him the finger.

"Saw that!" he yelled.

Since solving the case last season in Matlacha, after Hawk's course, I'd not only learned how to treat this work as a business, I also honed my PI skills. I could now identify owners of cell phone numbers, find out vehicle registration info, and knew how to acquire detailed and precise criminal records that a novice could get on the Internet.

Before the stalker had entered my life, I planned to learn how to do bug sweeps of homes and cars and how to monitor GPSs. But with each day of feeling watched, I withdrew. My motivation level to create or to hone my sleuth skills plummeted.

This was the first time I would put the new knowledge to work. I admitted, doing so almost made me want to paint a shingle: Jessie Murphy: Artist Sleuth at Your Service.

Almost.

10

Zen was right where I expected her to be, on the back dock of Bert's inhaling the smoke of other smokers. Vicarious nicotine hit. The choice of many born-again non-smokers.

She spotted me as I came through the door. "Hey, girl. I saw you leaving with John Boy. Wondered what you were up to." She finished her beer in one gulp.

"Tobin Peterson, that Walton John Boy?"

She shrugged and winked at me. "Everyone in Matlacha has another handle, girl, including Tobin Peterson. Want to know what yours is?"

"More info than I want to know, I suspect. Got time to talk?"

But I knew what it was: Quickwalker, a woman sidestepping a long-term relationship faster than a landed crab scurries toward the water.

"I always have time for you, girl. Come on, let's go in. All this smoke makes my head throb."

We opened the door to a room where blue and green painted beams were lined with license plates of several states, stuffed animals, lit beer signs, and stickers. Smells of homemade chips and fried fish hovered over the raw plywood floor. A dreadlock-adorned calypso musician's drumming brought a hush over the room.

Bert's Bar was a legend in Matlacha. According to the menu (the best way to get credible facts), the original building was built in the `30s as a "sweet shoppe." In `41 the "hotel" was built. During WWII soldiers from the base at Page Field in Fort Myers were frequent visitors of the hotel and hotel bar that had a reputation of ill repute. After the war it became known as "Mother's" and then as Harry's Barge Inn. The hotel operated until the early '80s. When a guy named Bert Clubb, a famous Lee County bar operator, purchased the place, it was named "Bert's." And Bert's it was to this day.

I liked to imagine it back in those days when shrimp boats were parked out back and dancers weaved through the tables much as Zen and I were doing right now—although we were not so evocatively dressed.

I raised my voice. "I see they have a male waiter, a new musician, and a couple of younger, prettier waitresses, but since last season, this place is the same."

Sliding onto the stool Zen signaled for two beers. "Changing Bert's would be like changing from a soft bra to an underwire."

I gave her my "I can't wait to hear the punch line" look.

"Like asking for bra entrapment." Zen's hoot of laughter was so loud she made the guy who sat next to her jump and spill his beer.

I merely shook my head. Zen could be real funny. And Zen could be real unfunny. This time she was the latter.

Grinning, the bartender set two Guinnesses on the counter.

"So you finally switched to a decent beer?" I looked at her over my raised glass.

Zen wiped tears from her eyes and grabbed her mug. "Making more bucks helps." Her expression sobered. "What's up? You look like yesterday's breakfast."

I told her about the resurrected stalker, the whereabouts of Gar and my conversation with Stoner.

"So, Jessie Murphy is sleuthing again?"

"Something like that." We clicked our bottles together. "So you'll help me, right?"

Zen glanced around. The table for two near the far door was free. "Let's go over there."

I nodded at several familiar faces as we zigzagged through the crowd. Pool balls cracked, drowning out the basketball game on TV. We sat. I placed my forearms on the sticky table, grimaced and removed them. Zen motioned to a waitress to wipe it off. When it was clean, I returned to my former comfortable position: arms on wooden surface, bottle of Guinness nestled in both hands.

Zen refused to look at me. Puzzled, I pushed up my tan cap and waited for her to begin. The door behind us opened. A cool breeze crossed over my neck. I raised my beer bottle as Zen began to talk.

"Uh, well, I have to say, I ain't so keen on the possibility of brushing noses with the law right now." She looked behind her. I got the feeling she was concerned someone had heard us. This wasn't like Zen. She was always up for investigative work. I frowned and took a long drink.

"You know I'm with a new squeeze, right?"

"Sure. The tourist."

"Well, he uh, well, he's kind of an important person and well, it wouldn't be good right now if I got into any trouble. He . . ."

I stopped her by raising my arms. "Got it," I said. "End of conversation. Pretend you never heard me."

She looked sheepish. "You understand, right? Any other time and I'd . . ."

"Got it, Zen. No apologies necessary." I stood. "Later." And, not wanting to say something I'd regret dropped my payment on the table, I shimmied through the door.

I was hurt and upset and Zen knew me well enough to know it. A man coming between us? Someone she would probably know a month, two if they were lucky? Now, when I needed her most to bolster my battered sense of who I was? NOW?

In the past Zen and I had been kind of an off-beat Yin and Yang team. I didn't know that many women in town. Lil had moved to Key West. Rose and Taco were in prison. Seems half the women I knew in Florida were crooks, except Zen and Lil of course. I needed to meet more women down here. Make more friends. I should become a Matlacha Hooker. When I first heard the name I was aghast. Who wouldn't be? Then I read they were a community outreach group whose originator had had a powerful sense of humor, thus the name. I wiped off my tears, gnawed on my lower lip, and smelled a familiar rancid smell.

"Nice night," Gator said.

"Don't you ever take a shower?" I regretted my rude words before he had time to absorb them.

"Good to see you again too. Welcome back to Matlacha."

We grinned at each other.

"Zen says you'd like to see me."

I blinked several times, then gazed back toward Bert's.

"She said that?"

I scanned Gator's aging bod. His hair was pulled back into a graying ponytail and he had wrapped his head in a red bandanna. He wore a filthy white muscle shirt. His chest hair was curly, matted and gray and seemed to be covered in dust. His cut-off jeans were coated with bait slime. His blue faded plastic flip flops looked like they were on their last day. His smell was so strong and repugnant it was all I could do to stand my ground.

But two things I knew. Gator could talk a blue streak when he wanted to. No one could get away from him. He could keep someone occupied longer than a cute Endo specialist. This trait just might come in handy. And as a long-standing local he knew almost everyone in town or knew someone who did. He was an eyesore, a welcomed eyesore.

Without further forethought, I stepped forward and hugged him, which took him and me off-guard, of course. I mean . . . eww.

A nearby fisherman sent up a mating call. Embarrassed and already sorry for the spontaneous action, I stepped away, dusted off my arms and hands and thought about taking a shower and buying some flea killer. I'd already begun to itch.

Gator chuckled. His eyes sparkled. He touched his bare arms where mine had been. "Investigative work, huh?"

I didn't want to imagine what he might be thinking.

I gave him a stern look. "Could be labeled by the wrong people upstairs as "Stay off our turf stuff.""

Gator rolled his head on his narrow shoulders. "I hate labeling, don't you?" A smile played on his lips.

A Coast Guard cruiser motored past. Gator waited for it to get under the bridge directly below us, then spit.

"The job pays twenty bucks an hour."

He took what looked like a coffee stirrer stick off his left ear and began to clean under his fingernails. I told him we would be going to see Rooster's ex in the morning.

On the way home I texted Hawk my news. I was as excited as a bride at her wedding: *I did it how you said. Fees, contract, and all!! Whoohee!!!*

I got the following message back: *You get a Florida license? Without it, you get caught and you could be barred from the profession or fined or both. Takes 8–12 weeks to process.*

Great. Just great.

Another text came in: *Don't put the horse before the cart without hookin 'er up.*

I typed fast: *hahaha. HA!*

Return text: *Sooo much like you, JESSIE!!!!*

I gave my ponytail a toss.

11

Bent over, hands on knees, I caught my breath. Those who think power walking isn't strenuous, have never done it. My hair was plastered to my head. My heart was a sump pump emptying out a flooded basement. I swiped my brow with the back of my hand and felt someone behind me. Saw white boots before I straightened and turned. Stoner Taylor. Cash in hand. No envelope. No protective plastic bag. Cold hard cash.

I shook my mop of hair like a wet otter, thinking about how I should approach the subject of my not being a professional private eye with a license in Florida. I had considered seriously not broaching it, but that didn't seem wise. The direct, honest approach seemed my best option. I did not reach for the cash. "Listen, one thing. I'm no professional PI. I don't carry a license in Florida. Understand?"

"And I take cash for most of my bait and don't declare it at tax time. So?" He extended his arm and offered me the cash. "We all have ta do what we have ta do." Wondering what else he did that he just had to do, I thanked him and stuffed the bills into my waistband.

"I've hired Gator as my partner," I said.

"I heard."

Of course he had.

"Good choice."

I had him come with me to the inn to ask him more questions. He sat on a deck chair. I fetched my iPad. He lit up a cigarette immediately. I made sure his smoke drifted downwind.

I learned Stoner had known Rooster since kindergarten. He acquired his nickname after he took a rooster to school in first grade for Show and Tell and demonstrated how the bird balanced itself on his arm. And here I thought it was because of his hairdo! The boys graduated in 1964. Rooster joined the Marine Corp right after high school and fought in Vietnam. He came back with a head injury and married his high school sweetheart. She died at age twenty-four of breast cancer. His second wife left him for a trucker.

Sadi Henning was Rooster's third ex-wife. They had two kids. She had moved from Mississippi to Punta Gorda five years ago with Rooster. The following year she divorced him. Months later she suffered a stroke. To Rooster's credit, he'd moved back in to nurse her and take care of the five and three-year-old. Sadi was only twenty-two.

"You said Rooster had worked for a school district before he was laid off. Know where?"

"The middle school in Punta Gorda."

"What did he do for them?"

"Janitor. Oh, they had some fancy different PC title all right, but he was a janitor. No getting around that."

I'd been typing steadily on my iPad while Stoner talked. It would have been wiser to use my tape recorder, but I hadn't thought of it soon enough. I'd left it in the room.

"Know where he lived?"

"With Sadi." He tossed his cigarette butt into the pass.

"Okay, yeah, sure, I meant the address."

"Hmm . . . went up there a couple of times. Can't remember the house number, but it's in the Gulf View Mobile Park off Burnt Store Road. Street's called Chariot something.

Real clean place. Like a vacation home. I was real proud of Rooster when I saw how he was taking care of his family."

"So, what kind of guy was your friend?"

"Ah, he was an upright guy. Didn't even smoke. If it weren't for the drinkin`, you'd think he was an angel."

"Yet he was smuggling pot."

"Ah, come on, anyone with a brain knows pot should be legalized. It has been in several states. It's just a matter of time before it'll be legalized everywhere. Hear how much money the state of Colorado is making from taxing it? Hell, every state should follow suit. America would be better off. Rooster was a man trapped behind the eight ball. He was a man before his time, that's all."

I would have expected no other opinion from a man nicknamed Stoner.

I sat back in my chair. "Okay, that's enough for now. I'm sure I'll have more questions later."

"You know where to find me."

We stood.

Stoner pulled another cigarette out of his pack and a joint fell onto the dock. He glanced at me and bent down. After picking it up, he reinserted it and walked away. At the corner of the inn, he hesitated and turned. "Know where I got my nickname?"

I shook my head.

"Brick mason. And a damn good one." He winked and disappeared around the building.

Oh, sure, I believed him. Absolutely.

At first I thought I wouldn't take Gator with me to see Sadi, but then changed my mind. Something told me that he would be a big help in getting her to open up to me. Two heads, Grandma always said, were better than one.

I found Sadi's number by using my old standby, switchboard.com. Sadi was willing to see me at 10.

I phoned Gator and asked him to meet me at 9 at the Bridgewater. Punta Gorda was less than a half hour away.

I drank two cups of coffee and ate a breakfast bar, then showered and dressed in jeans and a gray T-shirt, choosing my black flip flops and of course my tan cap for luck. Two seasons ago when I had overpowered Will's killer, I had worn these flip flops and tan cap on the night I nailed the woman.

I'm Irish and as superstitious as my Grandma Murphy, but tried to hide it more than she did. Before she moved to be by my mom and me in Boston, she'd lived in a small New England village, and because of her superstitious ways and beliefs people there got in the habit of calling her a witch. Although she knew they were only joking, she said that kind of talk made her nervous and she didn't like the idea of being dunked into a barrel of water to confess her sins. She was no tea bag, she said.

I was standing at my car when Gator appeared. Perhaps it was the realization that he was going to be a paid assistant to a sleuth, or perhaps he had been hit by lightning during the early morning thunderstorm, but what I saw almost made me inhale a swarm of gnats. Gator was clean shaven and his face although grooved with deep wrinkles was as smooth and shiny as a babe's. A Tommy Bahama hat sat rakishly on his head. He was just this side of handsome in a sixty-plus, backwoods sort of way. His clean white shirt looked like it had been ironed. The sleeves were rolled up and the shirt was tucked into a new pair of Levi's. Leather sandals completed his disguise. Dial soap and baby powder? Did I smell those? Oh, my!

"You can shut your mouth now," he said, opening the door and sliding onto the passenger seat.

I looked around to make sure I was in Matlacha and that I stood in front of the Bridgewater and that this was really Gator who climbed into my car. A pelican landed on a piling. An osprey swept past. Adjusting to my shock, I climbed in. "You clean up real good." I handed him the packet of information I'd printed off my iPad.

To my surprise, I had been unable to find info on Rooster, but his ex-wife had a clean record. Two credit cards maxed out. Thanks to Obama-care, she had health insurance.

I'd also done a background check on Stoner. He had two DUIs, but nothing more serious. Sixty-seven. Married once. Two kids. Debt-free, including his house, two cars, a new boat, and the bait shop. Pretty surprising for a man whose income came from one bait store. I figured Rooster must be within two years of Stoner's age.

Gator flipped through the pages, then set the folder and his hat on the dashboard.

"What do you know about Stoner Taylor?" I asked.

He reached into the door pocket. "Not much. He settled in Matlacha, oh, been about ten years ago I guess. Married a Pine Island crabber's daughter. Had their first kid four years back. His wife is in her early twenties.

"Seems Stoner and Rooster like younger women."

"Who doesn't?"

I let that pass. I'm twenty-nine. One more year and I wouldn't fit the younger woman category. Or perhaps by these men's standards, I didn't already. Whatever.

Holding up a plastic toy whistle, Gator smiled. "What's this?"

"One of my travel toys."

He grinned and began to play a tune.

"Okay, okay. Listen up. We're working here."

Giving one final loud toot, he returned it.

"Stoner got any bad habits other than drinking and pot?"

Gator gave me a sharp look. I told him about the joint that had fallen out of his cigarette pack. Gator shrugged. "Likes to play poker. Has a regular Saturday night group. But they don't play for high stakes."

"Did Rooster play with them?"

"Suppose so."

"You know the other players' names?"

"Nah, just heard they played. You got any more toys?"

I pulled out a sport whistle from the driver door pocket and handed it to him. "Is Stoner a churchgoer?"

Turning the red whistle this way and that, Gator nodded and slid it in his pocket, the same one that held his pack of cigarettes. "Just might come in handy later. And yeah, I hear he and the Missus go pretty regular."

Eyeing his bulging pocket, I said: "Don't forget who that belongs to."

"Don't worry. I'm not in the habit of stealing kids' toys." He smirked.

I gave him Grandma Murphy's evil eye. "Does Stoner have any other family down here?"

He grinned and patted his pocket. "Not that I know of. Kind of sweet to think of a PI who plays with toys."

I sighed but in all other ways ignored his comment. "I assume you met Rooster?"

"Yeah, sure, he usta hang around. He and Stoner were real tight."

The way he said it made me wonder. I glanced at Gator, eyebrows raised.

He caught my eye. "Well, let's just say I never knew buddies to be so, well, so insular when they were together, if you know what I mean."

"I'm not sure I do."

"Well, it's hard to explain exactly. It was like when they were together they had a secret pact no one could penetrate. Like it was just the two of them against the world. Rooster was smarter than Stoner, but never let Stoner or most others know it."

"Stoner said his friend was afraid. You know anything about that?"

"I knew something was buggin` him."

I let up on the gas and looked into the rearview mirror. Had that car been following us? I frowned.

"How so?"

"Talked to him on the bridge one night while we was both fishin`. We was talkin` about high school days and how teens do dumb things and all. Anyways, I was talkin` about that. He wouldn't keep his line in the water. Hell, I told him, you won't catch no fish doin` that all night. You know that."

"And?"

"It was his eyes . . . when he looked at me. Shiny as glass marbles. Looked like a deer in headlights. I was eating a package of fresh strawberries and offered him one. He said he was allergic to strawberries, hauled in his line and took his bucket and left. Don't think he liked my conversation."

I pressed down on the accelerator and glanced again into the rearview mirror. "That car was behind us in Matlacha. I'm sure of it." I'd turned onto Burnt Store Road.

"Looks like we got us some new friends," Gator said. "Put the pedal to the metal, gal."

Now, I'm not one for speed and I sure don't see me racing down a two-lane road trying to shake another car when a bicyclist could pull out at any minute. "You watch too many cop shows."

I pressed my foot on the brake and pulled over to the side of the road. The other vehicle passed. The driver was a woman and she was talking on her cell phone. She seemed to not notice us as she took the corner.

"A coincidence," I said.

Gator didn't hide his look of disgust. Obviously I'd insulted his thirst for high-speed adventure. "You ain't no fun."

12

We arrived at Sadi's home by 10. To park in the graveled parking space I had to drive over a curb. The house was a double-wide with a small, but inviting front porch. White spindles surrounded gangly hibiscus in bad need of pruning. A rusty, old-fashioned trike that looked like it had come from Goodwill sat near the front door. Two kids were shoveling sand into yellow and pink buckets in a sandbox at the rear of the house. Assuming an adult was nearby, I went that way. Gator followed as a radio switched on and Garth Brooks` voice added edge to the sultry air.

"Hate country music," Gator grumbled.

The lawn was almost devoured by leafy blades of Creeping Beggarweed, Dollarweed, and stems of sharply pointed, wilted Cat's-ear Dandelions. Numerous patches of dead areas looked like someone had gone slap-happy with Round Up, destroying healthy growth. Needle-sized sprigs of recently seeded silver-green grass looked as if they were struggling for life. Gator and I stepped around the new growth.

A truck drove past and backfired. I jumped and blanched. Knowing my stalker was still alive had me walking on a narrow emotional ledge again.

Sadi sat in a red and white webbed lawn chair watching her kids. When she saw us her expression changed from vacant to closed, to alert. The stroke had frozen the left side of her face and it appeared her left hand wouldn't uncurl. She held it in her lap, fingers up, as she reached out to take my outstretched one. Now she'd lost the man who took care of her. What a tough break.

After we introduced ourselves, Gator went under a nearby ficus tree and fetched back two more lawn chairs. The kids now stood protectively on either side of their mom. The girl wore a pink and white bathing suit. The boy, black swimming trunks. They were about four and six years old. The boy had dark tight curly hair, deeply tanned skin, and large round eyes that seemed to warn us not to upset their mother. The girl had carrot-red hair and bright, watchful eyes. Seemed like they'd dealt with more than most kids their age should have to.

"We were so sorry to hear about Rooster," I said, feeling awkward and almost ashamed that my body was whole and in working order.

Sadi blinked rapidly but said nothing.

"I don't know if you've heard, but Rooster's friend, Stoner Taylor has hired me, or us, to help find his killer."

For a moment I thought Sadi's hearing had also been affected as she didn't show any reaction or response. I opened my mouth to repeat myself, but Sadi spoke up.

"Thought it was a robbery."

Apparently her speech hadn't been affected by the stroke. At least she had that.

"The cops don't think so. Nothing was taken."

Sadi looked at the ground for a long time before she said, "He shouldn't have been there."

"In the bait shop?"

She caught my eye, touched her left cheek with her right hand and looked down quickly. "You're real pretty. I usta be pretty. Men called me a looker." Her voice trailed off. I didn't know what to say. She turned abruptly to her kids. "You two go back to that box. Hear me? Go on. Go play."

75

The boy gave me a stern, warning look and shuffled away. The girl followed.

"Cute kids," I said.

"He was supposed to be here. I'd made a berry pie. His favorite. Strawberry."

"So, you were expecting him?"

Her attention was on her kids. "I've already told this to the cops. He called to say he'd be a little late. I even bought ice cream." Her eyes filled with tears.

"Stoner said he planned to bring him home."

She glanced at me, then at Gator. "That Stoner. Didn't know Rooster was doing anything ille . . ." Her voice trailed off. "He never called again."

"You didn't try to call him?"

"Of course I did. But he never answered. Half the time he never answers his phone. The fool." Her eyelids fluttered.

"Stoner said lately he was scared of something or someone. Know anything about that?"

Sadi's fingers tightened on the arm of the chair. "Lately? Rooster always watched his back. Always."

"You mean he was always scared?'

She nodded. "Since I've known him."

"How long was that?"

"Seven years or thereabouts."

"And he was always scared?"

She nodded again. "Anyone who was friends of Rooster knew that he always watched his back. Stoner especially. They are, were, since they were kids in Mississippi . . . like Robin and Superman. That's where Stoner and I met . . . Mississippi."

"Stoner watches his back too?"

76

She shot a glance toward Gator. "She ain't the brightest penny in the bucket, is she?"

Gator chuckled. "There's duller ones, I reckon."

I gave him a look. He snickered and looked away.

I didn't keep the edge out of my voice. I didn't like being made fun of. Ever. "I was just making sure I understood you," I said, not hiding my irritation. She sniffed. I zipped my temper. One doesn't have to like someone even though they feel sorry for them. "Would you mind giving me a list of names of friends and acquaintances of Rooster's?"

She kept her eyes on the ground. "That's easy. There's me. Stoner, his poker buddies and his sister, Ellie George. She lives in Fort Myers. You can find her number in the phone book. She's some kind of high falootin' person or something. I never met her."

"That all?"

"Rooster wasn't a social moth. Oh, but he did work with teens at the Baptist Church in Punta Gorda and take yogi classes from some instructor he met there. You could talk to them and his instructor, I suppose."

"So he was a youth counselor?"

She shrugged.

"Know the pastor's name?"

"Kennedy."

"Did Rooster have many hobbies?"

"Hobbies? Never thought of Rooster with those things, but fishin', poker, and yogi, of course. He said yogi helped him sleep."

Seemed apt that this gal didn't know that yogi was the teacher and yoga the practice. She'd probably never practiced yoga.

"So he had trouble sleeping?" I asked.

Her eyelids fluttered. "Who doesn't?"

She had a point.

"What I meant was, do you think his sleeping problem had anything to do with his fear?"

Sadi looked at Gator again. "Do I look like some kind of psychologist?" She turned to me. "How the hell would I know?"

Gator shifted in his chair. I glared at him. If he chuckled again, I would fire him, right here and now. But instead, Gator surprised me by asking the next question. "Do you know the name of his instructor or any of the kids he worked with?"

"Nah."

"You have no idea who might have wanted to kill him?" Gator asked.

So when had he learned what questions to ask? Watching *Criminal Minds*?

"Nah," Sadi said.

I leaned forward. "Any idea of what or who he was afraid of?"

"Nah."

"He never talked in his sleep or gave any hint?" I asked.

"Nope, nothin`."

Gator gave me a look that said "Listen to this" and continued the interview. "Just curious. What brought you and Rooster to Florida? Mississippi is one fine state. I'd think it would be hard to leave."

That was a question that hadn't occurred to me. I admit, I was kind of impressed with the old goat.

Sadi gently touched her nerve-damaged cheek again. "Rooster said fewer people would know him here. He was tired of people. He just wanted to be left alone."

"Tired of people? But you said he worked with youth at the church, didn't you?" I asked.

"Yeah. Could never quite figure out Rooster. He was a surprise-a-minute kind of guy. In fact, the last time we were together I would have sworn it weren't . . . But, well, guess our private life ain't none of your business."

"Mind if I ask what decided you two to get unhitched?" Gator asked.

Sadi pushed back against her chair and looked up. It was a clear, cloudless day. "I got a voice. I wanted to go to Nashville, leave the kids with Rooster and make something of myself."

"And Rooster didn't want that?" I asked.

"Ah, he was okay with it."

"But you divorced," I said.

She blushed. "There was this guy . . ." Her voice drifted away again.

Gator and my eyes locked. A man with a motive.

"Was there a confrontation between him and Rooster?"

"Nah, they never met."

Sure they hadn't.

"Would you mind giving me his name? We need to cover all the bases."

Looking at me sharply, she mumbled. "Jake Lesan. But like I said, they never met."

"Know where he lives?"

"Not no more." She looked toward the sandbox and smiled a crooked smile.

I followed her gaze.

The girl held a full bucket of sand over the boy's bowed head. "Don't," he said through clenched teeth.

"Ada!" Sadi said in a warning voice.

Staring into her mother's eyes, the girl tipped the pail. The boy yelled, shot up and pushed his sister into the sand. She howled.

"Sometimes life's like that. Being defiant or being different is the only thing that can make you happy in the moment," Sadi said to us. "Rooster was just one big kid." She raised her voice, "Ada, you go over to that step and sit yourself down. Don't get up `til I tell you to." The child grinned as she wobbled toward the step. And she was only four. She was going to have a long, pot-hole road to travel.

Sadi moistened her lips. "People got to learn there are consequences to their actions. Rooster should have been here. He loved strawberry pie." She touched her cheek again and lowered her eyelids seemingly lost in mourning. The little girl leaned back against the step and gazed into the sky.

I looked around. What was Sadi holding back? I knew there was something, but I also sensed she had nothing further she would say. My eyes landed on the trailer.

"Do you mind if we go inside and look around?"

Her eyes widened. "Why?"

"There might be something inside that would give us a clue about Rooster that would help us. We know very little about him."

"The cops already did that. You won't find anything, I . . . maybe I should come with you," Sadi said gazing off in the distance.

"Totally up to you," I said, watching her closely.

She looked at Gator, at me and then shrugged. "There's a picture of him on the table by the door. You'll probably want one. Take it. I got more. His desk is in the bedroom. And take your shoes off."

I couldn't help but wonder what Sadi feared we would find as Gator and I headed toward the steps where the little girl was calmly having time out. I needed to expand Rooster's profile. Seeing where he lived would help. I reminded myself to ask two questions that Hawk said were important when viewing a victim's home, or when interviewing someone: What is it I can't see? And what does it have to say?

What couldn't I see from my exchange with Sadi? Well, I knew she wasn't being totally honest with me. People who are tired of other people don't get themselves entangled in numerous social activities involving kids. But, what had I not seen? I racked my brain for an answer but nothing came. I opened the trailer door and stepped over the threshold and . . . eww . . . Sadi's little girl began to SCREAM.

My fingers tightened on the doorknob.

Gator yanked my whistle out of his pocket, stuck it in his mouth and LET IT RIP.

13

Having accomplished his goal to distract and quiet the hysterical girl, Gator tossed me the whistle. We rushed inside as Sadi, left foot dragging, hurried as best she could to her. The child now held her hands over her ears, mouth clamped shut.

The house was surprisingly neat. Even the toys on the floor and a cardboard box of what I assumed were kid's dress-up clothes were positioned in a straight line against one wall. A 52-inch flat screen TV and a CD player on a makeshift shelving unit of bricks and varnished pinewood boards dominated the room. The books and CDs on the lower shelves had been shelved alphabetically. A variety of pillows filled one corner. A white rocking chair faced another overstuffed chair near a basket of various colors of yarn and knitting needles. The pine paneled walls were covered in perfectly aligned photographs.

I imagined Sadi with a measuring tape making sure each nail hole was lined up properly. In one picture Sadi, with a symmetrical face, was holding the baby girl. The boy stood beside her. Happiness and hope shone in Sadi's eyes. There were no pics of Rooster or any other man on the wall. I stepped back and using my phone took photos of the photos.

I walked in my bare feet to the table near the door and picked up the framed photograph of Rooster. He wore a white shirt opened at the neck. His hair was swept back behind his ears. His rugged handsome looks reminded me of a young

Mel Gibson. Gator had taken a seat in the rocker. I headed to the bathroom.

Feeling like a terrible snoop, but reminding myself that I was in the role of a private eye that required snooping, I opened the medicine cabinet. I learned that Sadi took sleeping and birth control pills, used Dial soap and liked Donna Karan Cashmere Mist deodorant, and that these shelves were as tidy as everything in the living room. Even the toothpaste was rolled up neatly from the bottom. The only other bottle in the cabinet was one of kids' vitamins. I closed the door, glancing at the waste basket. I picked it up, took a deep breath, and rifled through it. Crumbled up tissue. A half-eaten sucker. A toilet paper cardboard roll. I set down the plastic basket. As I straightened up, a light bulb went off in my head. I went to the sink and opened the medicine cabinet again. Odd. Not one item that showed that a man lived in the house. Rooster had been traveling, that was true. But would he really have taken all his toiletries? I frowned and headed for the bedroom.

Queen bed. Two nightstands. Desk. More photos of the kids. A print over the bed. An impeccably made bed. I opened the closet. Women's clothes. One hundred percent. I searched the shelf above, the floor beneath, but found nothing other than women's sweaters and shoes. I closed the door. No sign that Rooster had lived here. Very odd.

I sat at the desk. The blinds were closed. I switched on the desk lamp and lifted the blotter, but found nothing. Raised the lamp, nothing. I picked up the weighty cross hanging from a chain, then set it down again.

A black and white framed photograph of a man in sunglasses, white shirt and an expensive business suit sat in one corner. I took the picture out of the frame. The words Sam

Bowers Jr. were written in pen on the back. I returned the photo.

The drawers were empty. I turned in the chair and glanced at the print over the bed, then stood and went to inspect it more carefully. It was a realistic depiction of the inside of a bus with only one occupant—an African-American woman. It was unsigned. The print surprised me on two counts: One, it was quite good. Second, surely this was supposed to be Rosa Parks on the day she took a front seat to protest segregation. In the home of a white guy from Mississippi? There had to be a story here. One I wanted to hear and explore. I snapped two photos and went to the kitchen. Neat as a pin. I opened the fridge. My eyes landed on an uncut berry pie. I shut the door and went back to the living room, getting there just as Sadi and the kids entered. She did not look up. After she settled the boy and girl at the small table in the kitchen with cookies and milk, I asked her about the absence of Rooster's things.

She bit her lip before she answered. "After hearing the news, I haven't slept. I had to do something to keep from climbing the walls. I boxed them." Tears moistened her eyes. "Is that bad of me?" Her voice was a pitiful squeak.

I assured her that everyone reacted differently to sudden loss. I asked what she had done with them.

"Goodwill," she said. "Except for what's on the desk. I'm keeping those things. The cops took nothing, not even his picture."

"Everything else is gone?" I asked.

She pursed her lips and nodded.

I gave her some time to collect herself before asking about the print.

"Ah, that. Rooster was real attached to it. I don't plan to ever get rid of that either. Hey, watch your glass," she said to her son who had shoved it near the edge of the table, away from the busy hands of his sister.

"Did he say what meaning the picture had for him?"

"Nah, Rooster wasn't much of a talker." Her words caught in her throat. She turned her back to me. I wondered what words, what truths, hadn't been spoken by Rooster and by Sadi.

I'd questioned her enough for the time being. I said my farewells and went into the living room. As I did, another piece of Hawk advice telegraphed through my mind: Always look for something that doesn't fit in with the rest. What hadn't fit in? The image of the woman on the bus. And there was something else, but I couldn't put my finger on it.

"Ready?" I said to Gator who apparently had not moved from his comfortable seat.

"Sure." He pushed himself upright.

Outside, the temp had risen at least twenty degrees.

"Was the rocker comfortable?"

"Not so much."

I frowned and glanced his way. His lips twitched and his eyes sparkled with mischief. "You found something?" I asked.

He hurried ahead, climbed into the car and slammed the door. More than curious, I followed, turning to him before putting the key in the ignition.

"What?"

Smiling a shit-eatin' grin, he unbuttoned his shirt and pulled out a white piece of fabric, then spread it across his lap. "Found this in the kid's play box."

Eyes wide, I stared at a pointed, white hood with two round holes for eyes.

"The Klan?"

"Ain't no Halloween costume, I reckon."

The front door of the trailer opened and Sadi appeared. Gator stuffed the hood under his seat.

"Hey," I started the engine. "you can't take stuff from someone's house. That's stealing," I said, putting the car in reverse.

Gator, eyes on Sadi, who apparently was returning to the yard with her kids, shrugged. "Got me a thing about Halloween. That's what I'd tell her." He sniffed. "If I'm asked of course, which I won't reckon I will be."

"There was a cross on a chain and a realistic print of an African-American woman on a bus in the bedroom."

"Click. Click. Click," Gator said.

I was really starting to appreciate this old codger. He was much cleverer than he let on. I nodded. "If my memory serves me right, it was around `65 when Mississippi was deep into the segregation business. I'm thinking that would be about the time Rooster and Stoner would have been in high school."

"A sick time," Gator said.

"We need to collect some facts."

He scratched his ear and looked my way. "How will ya go about doin` that?"

"My ex-boss, Hawk, has contacts all over the U.S. I'll call in a favor, then I'll start my own research on the web."

Gator grinned. "This here is real fun work as far as work goes, not that I'm much into work, mind you," he said. "But a little can't hurt you too much, I reckon."

I pulled out my notebook and found the page with Rooster's sister's name, took out my cell phone, switched on the web, and went to switchboard.com. Eleanor George lived off Winkler in Fort Myers. Her phone was unlisted.

"Let's go see if Rooster's sister is home," I said. "She has to have plenty of information about her brother."

I wasn't that hopeful that Eleanor George would be honest with us, but I needed to get some straight answers about Rooster and his possible connection with the Klan. Fast.

14

My GPS led us to a gated community with an open gate that I slid right through. The townhouses and single-family homes probably ranged from 300k to millions. No Creeping Beggarweed or Cat's-eye Dandelions survived long in these manicured lawns.

"These places give me the jitters," Gator said.

"Why?"

"Too damn perfect."

I leaned forward and looked around Gator. "This is it," I said as I turned onto a brick driveway and Gator whistled.

"Not bad," he said.

The house had to be worth a mil at least. Not bad indeed.

"Don't steal anything," I said as I parked. "These places are high on security."

Gator chuckled. "Suppose I can smoke inside?"

"Yeah, right."

An elderly woman with white hair who looked to be in her late eighties opened the door. Thinking of my grandma, I introduced ourselves. She said Mrs. George was home and if we'd wait a minute she would see if she was accepting visitors. She walked away.

Gator reached toward an etched glass vase on a round table in the center of the hallway. I smacked his hand. "Keep your hands to yourself," I said in a harsh whisper.

His eyes sparkled with mirth as he stuck his hands in his pockets.

The woman returned.

We followed her into a white and pale-blue living room that made me feel as if I'd stepped into a cloud. White upholstered sofa against the wall, facing the entrance. Two matching chairs. Oriental rug. Round white coffee table. Glass vase shaped like an urn filled with white flowers. Intimate, inviting—very feng shui.

I sat beside Eleanor. She smelled like gardenias. Eleanor George's voice was refined, almost formal in an upper class, southern aristocracy type way. It was obvious by how she held her head and the vacant appearance of her eyes that she was blind.

Gator hesitated at the two white chairs.

"Do sit," she said, smiling. "Please." Her tone was polished and deep with a radio announcer's power.

Gator sat on the edge of one chair.

"Mrs. George…" I began.

She interrupted, "Eleanor, please."

A tiny cynical utterance in my head said this woman was quite an actress, faking this gracious, refined woman role. After all, she was Rooster Henning's sister, right? But looking at her, I had the stronger feeling that the voice in my head was wrong. I gave her our condolences for the loss of her brother. She turned toward the window before accepting them. I feared she might break down and cry. Softly I told her who I was. She blinked.

I leaned forward and spoke firmly. "Eleanor, we are hoping that you can tell us something about your brother that could help us nab his killer. I assume you've talked to the police?"

"Michael, my husband, did. I haven't yet. I'll miss Jonah. He was a loyal, loving brother."

"Were you close?"

She sighed, then nodded. "Not for years, but we were together at least once a week since he came to Florida." She smiled a sad smile. "I'm eighty-eight. Being reunited with my younger brother after so many years meant a great deal to me. We were many years different in age, but we had once been close."

"So you had been estranged?"

"Oh, yes. He left home right after high school and never returned. Even though I was married by that time, I missed having him in my life."

I felt my heart soften toward this woman. "So you were raised in Mississippi too?"

"Yes, of course. Jonah and I had the same father but different mothers. His mother was my father's second wife. Unfortunately, she died in childbirth. My father never got over her death and unfortunately he blamed . . . Before our father died, he made me sole beneficiary of his estate. I always felt badly about that. Thank goodness I could help Jonah's ex-wife during her tragedy."

"You met Sadi?"

"Oh, no. Unfortunately, not. But Jonah allowed me to write a check to help pay for her bills while she was convalescing. When he was younger, he refused to have anything to do with his father's money. Fortunately, age made him a wiser man. You should have seen him as a youth, he was quite the lady's man."

"Do you have any pictures of him when he was young? I saw a current one. He was quite handsome."

"No, unfortunately, there was a fire. So much was destroyed, including all photo albums and framed pictures, important documents. Such a shame."

I felt more and more kind-hearted toward this woman and was struggling with a way not to insult her when I asked if she thought her brother was a Klan member. I mean, it seemed so unlikely. I glanced at Gator. He was looking at me sternly. I bit my lip and he folded his arms over his chest and solved the problem.

"I found a Klan hood in Rooster's house. You know anything about him and the Klan?"

I blanched at the abruptness of the question and shot him a dagger. With hardened eyes, he continued to concentrate on Eleanor.

To my surprise, she smiled. "Jonah told me once his nickname was Rooster. How very sweet. He was always the sweet one. He . . ." Her sentence drifted away. She turned her head toward the window.

Gator and I waited for her to continue. But if Eleanor had heard the part about the Klan, she didn't let on. Instead, she put her hands in her lap and intertwined her fingers. I remembered my grandpa doing that often before he passed.

"Eleanor?" I said softly.

She blinked several times. "It's been years since . . . well, years . . . Mississippi was a long time ago. Such an awful time. Such terrible ignorance." She averted her head.

I touched her hand. "I'm sorry, I have to ask this. Was Jonah a member of the Ku Klux Klan?"

"Such terrible ignorance," she repeated.

A door opened and closed. The sound echoed over the white tiled floor as a tall, stout man with steel-gray hair entered the room. He took in Gator, me, Eleanor and frowned. "What's this?" he asked.

I told him who we were and why we had come, to get information that might help us find Eleanor's brother's killer.

He went to his wife and took her hand in his. The expression on her face was one of pure devotion.

"Then you know my wife is upset. To lose her only sibling in such a violent manner has been very trying. Please, do come back another time."

Eleanor seemed to disappear into the cushions of the sofa as her husband ushered us out of the room. At the front door, he lowered his voice. "My wife has been quite ill. She only last week came home from the hospital. She's heavily medicated and at times forgets what she wants to say." He reached for his pocket and drew out a business card. "Do phone me before you come again. Her family has been a cross for her to bear since she was born." He opened the door. "That brother of hers always had his hand out. He never left here without a check. I'm sure he had it tough as a kid, but you'd think he wouldn't want to take advantage of his sister in her old age."

"Maybe he thought some of that money should be his," Gator said.

The man's eyes narrowed.

"How long has your wife been blind?" I asked.

"More than twenty years now. Goodbye."

As we walked down the long flight of stairs, I said, "I think she was about to tell us something, don't you?"

"Might be."

"After the funeral, we'll talk to her again."

"Just remember, she ain't your grandma. Don't go easy on her."

I ignored his comment. But I knew what he meant. Because of her age and blindness, I would have a tendency to be too gentle, letting my emotions run the interview. Although

Gator's abrupt approach was off-putting, it got the job done, well had almost gotten it done.

"You know where the Baptist Church is in Punta Gorda? I'm thinking that's our next stop." While the startling Klan lead was compelling, I knew that I would need to do several hours research about that angle on my iPad and it would also take time for Hawk to get back to me. I wanted to talk to Rooster's preacher. Maybe he had confessed to some evil deed and his killer was an avenger.

"Me know where a church is?" Gator said, grinning.

I laughed again. Gator was fun to be around. He was no churchgoer, he assured me.

"I should have gotten the address from Sadi. Hopefully there's not two Baptist churches in Punta Gorda."

Gator pulled out his pack of cigarettes.

"Not in the car," I said.

He returned them to his pocket. "Speaking of being scared of somethin` . . ."

"Yeah?"

"What's got you spooked? You kept looking into the rearview mirror and stopping back there. You got a bug up your . . . Well, anyways, ain't no reason the killer would be after us, is there? I mean, you couldn't think he'd know this soon that we was after him?"

"No, it's not that." It was time to tell Gator about my stalker. He sniffed several times as I talked. I was surprised he wasn't aware of it. What with his being friends with Zen and Luke Abbot. Gator was surprised too.

"How come I never heard nothin` about this?" He rolled down his window. The air was deadly hot and humid. "Seems someone wanted me out of the loop." He stuck his head out, then pulled it back in and rolled the window up. Sweat beads had already popped out on my forehead. I turned up the air conditioner fan.

"Zen never let on," he grumbled.

"She's all google-eyed and distracted by a new guy," I said.

He scratched the top of his head. "You met him?"

"Nah, but I saw him once," I said. "He's too fancy for Zen, but she'll learn that fast enough."

"Maybe it'll work out."

"Yeah, and maybe we'll have an earthquake tonight."

I didn't want to openly agree with Gator, but silently I did. Zen was focusing so hard on this new guy, nothing else mattered. She would have to find the right path in her own time. I just hoped she wasn't hurt too badly in all the twists and turns or lost too many friends along the way.

I pulled into a Quick Trip and let Gator go in and ask for directions to the church. As it turned out, there were eight Baptist churches in Punta Gorda.

Great. Just great.

15

At each church we stopped at Gator opted to wait outside. Churches reminded him that he was a sinner, he said with a wink. I felt discouraged as I parked the car at the fourth one. This building was stark white and complete with a steeple. Again, Gator refused to come in. I slammed the car door extra hard.

I left him getting ready to light up, passing a sign that assured me that following Jesus was the ultimate adventure. My idea of "ultimate" had nothing to do with religion. Shoot me, but my afterlife wasn't that much on my mind and following any man, spiritual or not, just wasn't my style.

Stepping inside, I was shocked by the size and height of the sanctuary. The smell of jasmine from a nearby vase of flowers made me scratch my nose as I looked at the room that was as imposing as a clipper ship. The mast of a 70-foot sailing yacht would easily clear the beamed ceiling. Skylights and rows of windows let in the sun's rays. The front half of an octagon-shaped altar was accessed by three separate sets of stairs, four steps each. Rows of chairs faced each set of steps. A wall-sized stained glass window featured a Christ figure in a blood red robe. A large screen highlighted the back wall. Grandma's Catholic church, which I had faithfully attended as a kid, seemed modest in comparison. The room was so quiet and eerie that the skin on the back of my head began to itch. When I could paint again, I knew this scene, complete with the imagined yacht and its mast in the center, sails flapping, would be one of my subject matters.

"May I help you?"

I jumped and placed my hand over my heart. Far to the left a man's head appeared around a white four-foot wall. "You startled me," I croaked then moved down the aisle. I introduced myself and asked if this was Pastor Kennedy's church.

"Yep. He's in the community room—out the door, down the hall, first door to the left."

Bingo!

The man's head disappeared again.

I found Kennedy setting up tables and chairs. I told him who I was and asked if he'd mind answering some questions about Rooster Henning. His expression saddened when I said the name. We sat.

Kennedy had graying hair and . . . Whoa! Like WHOA! I sat up straighter. I hadn't had this happen since I first met my ex-beau, Will. Jay Mann, my second serious relationship, had been a slower start. What happened with Tobin was still to be seen. But, now? Hello libido!

I watched Kennedy closely under my lowered eyelashes as he talked.

"Jonah was a blessing to our church and congregation. He'll be sorely missed. It is difficult to believe that God sanctions such sudden loss, but one has to keep the faith, especially at times like this. God must have wanted Rooster for some other heavenly purpose."

Making a herculean effort to put aside my primitive sexual draw toward the pastor which threatened to turn me into a bimbo, I made myself concentrate on the business at hand, creating a profile of a murder victim, gathering leads to help find his killer. I tugged down my cap and made my voice have as tough an edge as I was capable of. "I understand he did quite a bit of volunteer work for you."

"Not for me, of course. I am merely a servant of the church and God. But, yes, he was a very active member. He loved to work with our young people. They love, er loved, him. Young African-Americans, and the majority of our young are African-Americans, don't always relate to Caucasian adults, but Jonah was an exception, a welcomed one."

I pulled my attention away from his sincere eyes. "What kind of things did he do with them?" I asked.

"Oh, taught Sunday school, chaperoned summer camp, helped organize Youth Work Day. That sort of thing. It was almost a calling for him—to help our youth get started down the right path."

A man who was tired of people?

"Would I be able to have a list of those he worked with?"

He frowned. "A list of our youth?"

I nodded.

"I, uh . . ." He shook his head. "I'm not comfortable giving out names without their or their parent's permission. I hope you can understand that."

He was right. It was a misguided request. I apologized and focused on a plaque on the wall behind his head: *You shall overcome*.

"I can let you talk to T-Strap. He's in the kitchen. That is, if he's willing to do it. He and Jonah were quite close. Shall I ask?"

"That would be great. If you don't mind?"

The pastor stood.

"Just a few more questions. Did Jonah ever speak to you about being afraid of something or someone?"

He sat again. "Why, no."

"Did he have any problem with anyone at the church that you know of?"

He ducked his head and concentrated on the faux wood. His action spoke volumes. Rooster *had* had problems. But when the pastor raised his head he denied knowing any such thing. Isn't lying a no-no for Baptists? Grandma Murphy would have definitely not approved, nor did I. I felt the invisible thread connecting him to me snap.

I cleared my throat. "I understand he took a yoga class sponsored by the church. Is it possible to give me the instructor's name and contact information?"

"That I can do," he said, seeming relieved.

I had no further questions, so Kennedy asked me to wait while he went to talk to T-Strap. While he was gone I thought about Will's belief in past lives. How he often talked about how souls left a body when a person died and entered another body in a new birth. I had always poo-pooed the idea, but what had just happened with the pastor got me thinking. What if we had known each other in a past life and our souls recognized each other? Had the pastor felt the same draw? A bizarre thought and one that didn't seem to help me one iota in the murder investigation. Besides, I don't start relationships with liars.

Ever. Period.

But my libido said, nonetheless . . . Ahh.

16

I felt Kennedy enter the room before I heard or saw him. He was accompanied by a tall teenager about fifteen or sixteen with an Afro hairdo striped with bright purple strands. The kid held a cell phone. His arms were tattooed in various intricate designs that appeared to be of African origin. He wore jeans and a muscle shirt. His grip was firm when we shook hands and were introduced.

"As I told you, son, Ms. Murphy is here to investigate Mr. Henning's death," the pastor said. "I'm sure she'd appreciate any help you can give her. Why don't you put your phone away?"

The teenager dropped it into his breast pocket.

"I'll leave you two to talk while I find the information you requested."

T-Strap followed the pastor's movement out of the room. The expression in his eyes was: Irritated? Angry? Once Kennedy was gone, he gave me a look that telegraphed "You bore me" and withdrew his phone and started playing a game.

I know a disgruntled teen with a chip on his shoulder when I see one. After all, I was once one.

"I'm sorry about your loss," I said. "Pastor Kennedy said you and Mr. Henning were close."

T-Strap shrugged and concentrated on his phone screen. "A private eye, huh? That must be a cool job," he muttered without looking up.

"Well, it's a part-time thing really."

He looked me up and down. "You get any training?" he asked. His fingers moved faster than a hummingbird's wings.

"On the job, so to speak and one course. You interested in criminology?"

He shrugged again. "Might want to be a cop someday."

I nodded. "A noble profession," I said, wanting more than anything to grab the phone and toss it in the waste can.

He rolled his tongue around the inside of his mouth, but didn't look up. "You watch *CSI* and *Criminal Minds*?" he asked.

"Oh, yeah." I thought about the times Grandma Murphy and I had watched the back-to-back series all evening, popcorn bowl between us, glasses of iced orange juice constantly filled. The fact that we'd seen each episode before didn't matter. The memory made me smile foolishly. T-Strap nailed me with an expression of disgust then resumed his game.

"Sorry," I said, "I was thinking of a time with my grandma. That's what happens when someone mentions those shows."

His facial muscles relaxed. He pocketed the phone. I felt like singing.

"I dig that. What'd ya need?"

"I need to get a picture of who Mr. Henning was. Anything you can tell me about him could be of help."

"You profiling him?"

"I guess you'd say that, yeah."

He reached toward his pocket, changed his mind and intertwined his fingers. "Rooster wasn't your ordinary white guy," he said. "He cared."

"I gathered that. How long have you known him?"

"Guess a couple years, since I was thirteen. That's when Mama and I started coming here. I got to be a youth counselor at camp that summer and he was one of the hot dog adults. Some of the olders were way too straight and hot into the Bible, but Rooster knew where it was at. He knew how to play the game right."

"Play the game right?"

"He didn't talk down to us or at us, he listened, man. He was rad," he said with a shaky, heated tone as he stared at the floor. In a lower voice he murmured, "Wish I hadn't been playing basketball when he was killed. If I'd been in that bait shop I woulda shot the other guy myself. "

So the kid just gave me an unasked for alibi on an offering plate. Interesting. Surely Rooster wasn't selling pot to these teens? Tell me he wasn't. Tell me this kid didn't kill him.

I paused to let T-Strap get his emotions under control before continuing. "Anyone you know dislike him?"

"Sure, man. *We* loved him. The pastor loved him, but plenty of the congregation didn't *like* him."

"Why?"

"Fear, man. They didn't trust him. Anyone who could get that close to us must be a pedophile. That sort of thing."

My eyes widened. I leaned forward. "Did anyone confront him with this?"

"Oh, yeah. There was even talk of calling the cops. They had a meeting to vote on whether to ask him to leave the church."

And Kennedy hadn't mentioned this? Whoa!

"How did Rooster take it?"

"What do you think? He was disgusted but he was cool about it. Never saw him riled up or nothing. Just said they were sick suckers."

101

"Who were 'they'?"

Our eyes locked. "Pastor Kennedy didn't tell you about this?"

I shook my head.

"Then neither did I," he said. Just like that, he shut down, pulled out his cell phone again, stood and walked out.

The room was so quiet I wanted to spit.

17

I got up and paced along the lines of tables and chairs. I wished I had Zen with me, but Zen was off shacking up with some guy. Zen would have come into the church and observed the two exchanges. We could have discussed what the next plan of attack should be. Gator was no team player. He was far too independent. I still wasn't very happy about him stealing that hood. I didn't need to be arrested for being a thief.

I was more than tired of people lying to me or just not telling the full truth. I was sick of being rational. I wanted to climb into a round tube at a water slide and in the tunnel scream as loud as I could all the way to the bottom.

Kennedy strolled in holding a piece of paper with, I assumed, the name and phone number I'd requested. He held it out, not knowing of course what T-Strap (where did he get such a dumb name anyway?) had just told me. Seeing Kennedy, thinking of his lack of integrity and still struggling against the incredible cosmic sensual pull, my desire to run home to paint turned into seething anger and disgust directed toward the pastor. I glared at him.

"We need to get something straight," I said. "Rooster has been murdered. I've been hired to help find his killer. Most murders are committed by someone who knows the victim. I just learned from a rude teenager information that could give me important leads that you obviously decided to keep from me. I don't think that's honest." I dug my toes into the rubber of my flip flops. Crossed my arms over my chest. Raised my chin another notch. Showing who was in control more than I felt.

Kennedy eased himself into a chair. "Ah, so the boy told you about the unfounded rumor and petition. Yes, well, it's true. I suppressed the information. Many people were upset by Jonah's closeness with the kids. Accusations were made, but the police were never involved. All this news about priests and abuse of kids. It's not surprising that witch-hunts happen. I tried to quell the rumors. Never did I believe them."

I placed my hands on my hips and spread my legs wide Spiderman style, again hoping the stance showed power. "I want the names and phone numbers of anyone involved," I said.

"But . . ."

I narrowed my eyes and interrupted him. "Is there a reason you're protecting them?"

He stood.

"Did you know that Jonah Henning was transporting marijuana the morning he was caught? Did you ever have an inkling that he might be selling it to the teens in your congregation?"

Kennedy's eyes went wide. He collapsed onto the chair he'd just left. "No! I . . . NO!"

I took a step forward. "Where were you the night Rooster was killed?"

"Why you don't think, you couldn't think that I . . ."

"Where were you, pastor?"

"I was with my wife all night. It was one of the few nights this past month I had to spend with her. She'll validate that."

I felt my heart trip over a tightrope. A wife! "Oh, I have no doubt she will," I said.

"This is ridiculous. I had no idea Jonah was involved with drugs. And I said nothing about the pedophile accusation because I thought with Jonah now in heaven there was no reason to continue to spread the false rumor. Surely, his ex-wife and children do not need to hear this. Surely, you don't think one of our parishioners would kill on unfounded accusations? That's not reasonable."

Who is this guy to tell me what's reasonable and what isn't? He certainly wasn't my mom, the woman who said this over and over again.

I kept my voice steady and calm. "Rage has little to do with reason, pastor. Rage is passion driven and can be truly dangerous. What if one of the kids Rooster was supplying got mad at him for whatever reason and lost his cool? The information?"

The pastor heaved a heavy, loud sigh and caved in like a line of dominoes: First, another sigh, then a quivering lip, a crestfallen face, slumped shoulders ending with pushing himself out of the chair. I followed him to his office where he compiled the list. When he handed it over, I read it carefully for missing details. 1. Roger and Sheila Turnstone, parents of Tim, age 15. Carpenter and social worker from Punta Gorda. 2. Cheryl and Joe Kirkpatrick, grandparents and guardian of fifteen-year-old Jake. 3. Mary Ellen Warner, single parent of Eddie, age 12. Operates a consignment shop in Punta Gorda. 4. Dave Kelly, single parent of sixteen-year-old Danny. Mechanic in Cape Coral. 5. Larry Cooper, single parent of Jed, aged 13. Yacht repair business at Burnt Store Marina, Punta Gorda. 6. Bev Seagate, yoga instructor. Each name came with a phone number and address. At least the pastor was organized.

My anger coupled with the tug of war between his spirit and mine, had made me sweat. I swore the air conditioner must have malfunctioned. The place was airless and still. I took off my cap and rubbed my forehead with the back of my hand.

"I need T-Strap's address as well."

He bowed his head, took the piece of paper and added it.

When I stepped outside, list in hand, Gator hurried over. "What happened to you? You look like you been to a water park on a blazin' hot day and didn't go in the water and have any fun."

I gave him a quick head shake and stomped past him. "Oh, shut up!" I said.

"Now you look like . . ."

I swiveled and stopped him cold with my meanest, Grandma Murphy "Say one more word and you're ground round" look.

As I settled in behind the steering wheel, I analyzed my anger. After all, it was an over the top reaction to the pastor, his lying and the kid's sudden shutdown. I should be used to people lying to me by now while I was in the role of a PI. But I wasn't. I'd been raised with certain expectations about who should be in touch with truth and honesty and even though the pastor's explanation was somewhat understandable, it didn't alleviate the disappointment that had led to my ultimate anger. And there was his "rational" comment. That, of course, had set me off. At times like this, I wished I were someone else, someone less emotional who had lower moral expectations and a different childhood. I'd probably live longer and definitely have fewer zits. I could already feel one developing on my right cheek.

Dang! I hadn't had sex in so long my body threatened to become an unleashed storm. Get control of yourself, woman!

Pastor Kennedy stepped out the front door and waved. Letting out a soundless growl, I started the car. Gator had still not climbed inside. I frowned and rolled down the passenger window. "What's the holdup?" I asked.

His gnarly face appeared. "Just waitin` for the cool-down."

I knew he wasn't talking about the temperature in the car, although it was hot as a pizza pan just taken out of the oven. I told myself to let it go. I took a deep breath and held it, then slowly exhaled. Did it again. And again, listening for the silence at the end of my breath. My neck muscles relaxed. My lower-body ache subsided. My heartbeat steadied. I looked at Gator whose expression was bemused. "Okay. Get in. I'm over it."

He opened the door. "So, what happened?"

I turned the key in the ignition and left out my overactive sexual yearnings as I filled him in. "And next time I interview someone, I want you with me. What do you think I'm paying you for, smoke breaks?"

"Roger that," he said. "What's next?"

"Although I'm itching to talk to those people who blackballed Rooster, I'm thinking it might be best to talk to his yoga instructor first. Agreed?"

I saw the surprise and pleasure Gator felt when I asked his opinion. He appeared to be stifling a grin and his shoulders straightened ever so slightly. "Sounds like a plan," he said.

18

Bev Seagate answered on the first ring and was willing to see us within the hour. Her yoga studio was in the unattached garage at her home. She lived in North Cape Coral. I hung up and added her address to my phone GPS.

A tall, thin, and most likely just over seventy woman met us at her front door. Two matching empty urns flanked her entrance. Knowing from Will that this was one way to welcome new opportunities into your life, I wondered what Bev was wishing for.

Inside, Gator and I sat on leather chairs. Bev lowered herself in the middle of a tan fabric sofa. The cherry coffee table was dominated by a black stone Buddha. A *Chutes & Ladders* kid game and a deck of *Old Maid* sat on a crossbar under the coffee table.

"That was Jonah's chair," Bev said, nodding toward Gator who seemed transfixed by the games. She faced me. "His spirit is with us today." Her voice was a whisper.

A breeze wafted through the window behind me, making the lace curtain gently touch my bare shoulder. I looked around, but saw no apparition. Ghosts I believed in. Had since I'd seen Grandpa's at the end of my bed less than a year after he had died.

It didn't seem appropriate to give my condolences when Jonah's ghost was most likely listening. Instead, I asked if she would tell us what kind of man Jonah was, after letting her know we had just left the church.

"Then you've heard about the dreadful accusations. Such a shame. Jonah Henning was a kind-hearted man with a gentle soul who wanted to give back to society. Those people should be ashamed of themselves."

I leaned back and nodded, noticing that Gator seemed preoccupied. These didn't sound like words from someone who might want him dead. But don't be a fool, I told myself. Lying convincingly was too often a well-honed skill.

She continued. "Jonah insisted that none of his friends go to that meeting. He didn't want anyone standing up for him. He said we shouldn't dignify their actions with our presence."

Aware that my ridiculous distraction with Kennedy had caused me not to ask all the right questions, I cautioned myself to be on the mark. I certainly didn't want Gator to lose all faith in me. I leaned close. "When was this meeting?"

"Three days before Jonah was . . . his spirit left his body."

"And the result?"

"Oh, they voted to ask Jonah to leave, but agreed there wasn't enough evidence to call the police. Apparently, those people did not believe in facts."

"Was Jonah aware of this?" I asked.

"Yes, he was told that very night."

"How did he react?"

"Much better than I would have. He came here to meditate."

"Did he plan to leave the church?"

Gator continued to eye the games. I figured he was daydreaming about a cig.

"The last I heard, he hadn't decided."

The pastor must also have known this. More information he'd kept to himself. His lying was beginning to look more than fishy. I told myself to be sure and have Hawk check him out.

Gator averted his eyes from the games and peppered Bev with a hard look, a hint that something besides having a smoke was brewing inside his head.

I gave him my shoulder. "We've been told that Jonah lived in fear. Do you know anything about that?"

"Well, yes, Jonah had serious issues with his past. That's what brought him to yoga and meditation, but he never shared that personal history with me. We spoke chiefly of spiritual issues. Once my sink stopped up and he came and replaced the pipe. He was like that, always there when he was needed. The children at that church worshiped him. He was always there for them. And, his ex-wife, poor thing. Have you met her?" I nodded. "Then you know about the stroke. Jonah always took care of her and those two darling children. He was a saint."

"Saints been known to bugger young boys," Gator said in a harsh, resounding intonation that seemed to make even the Buddha vibrate with surprise.

Bev blushed. I gaped at Gator.

Bev unfolded her legs. "Yes, unfortunately, that's true. I can only give you my opinion about a man I knew as a giving, kind individual."

Gator's expression remained hard and inflexible. "You got kids?"

"Why, no. Why do you ask?"

Gator's gaze landed on the games under the table. Bev looked at them, then at Gator. "I keep them for my niece."

Gator was thinking otherwise. Which made me doubly glad I insisted that he be present. While I had noticed the games, I hadn't drawn a conclusion from them, other than she

110

obviously had young people visit. Gator apparently had another idea. Great. It was time to bring up the pot connection.

"Did you know that Jonah was involved in transferring pot from one state to another?"

Her complexion turned a tad bit more whitish.

So she did.

The curtain fluttered again. I looked that way expecting to see Rooster's spirit pointing a gun at me.

Bev raised her head. "Actually," she said, "I did."

"You were aware that he was involved in drugs?"

She looked away. "I was aware that Jonah needed money to pay off his ex-wife's hospital and doctor bills. I was aware that he agreed to transfer a supply of pot. But please understand, for him this was a one-time thing. He told me what he was going to do the last time I saw him. And he swore he would never do it again."

"And you believed him?"

"Absolutely. I remember our conversation as if it happened this morning. I had made chocolate covered strawberries. When I offered him one, he said if he ate one he'd break out into hives. He confessed he felt compelled by God to help Sadi and his kids. His motive was pure. I felt sorry for him. Life, I assured him, isn't always fair. Sometimes we are forced to perform illegal acts to right wrongs. So sad."

"Knowing he might go to jail, did you try to talk him out of it?"

"Absolutely, but he wouldn't listen. I, of course, agreed with him that the government and laws and physicians and hospitals who charge such high fees for services are not in the right. Everyone knows that. It's been proven that marijuana helps ill people. How many states has its use been legalized in? What he was going to do was . . . well . . . not such a bad a thing to do."

"You think he supplied pot to the kids at the church?"

"Oh, absolutely not. Never! Jonah would never do anything to harm those kids."

"So he did think pot use was harmful?"

"To kids, yes. He didn't believe kids should use any drug, including alcohol. He was not a user himself. Ms. Murphy, this was a man trying to help his family get out of hard times. In my book, he was a hero."

"Did he tell you who hired him?"

She shook her head.

Gator caught my eye. His skepticism shown like a beacon.

The curtain swayed forward and backward. I rubbed my nose. "Where were you the night Jonah was killed?"

"Here alone."

Thus no alibi that could be corroborated.

"Well, okay, that's all I have to ask for now. If there's anything you've forgotten to tell us that you think would help, I'll leave my phone number."

She walked us to the door.

"Well, do you believe her?" I said to Gator after the door closed.

He took two more steps. "Don't trust her."

"Why?"

He shook out a cigarette and put it in his mouth, then took it out again. "Let's just say she reminded me of my aunt." He lit up. "My aunt made my folks' life hell. She also looked all innocent with her meditation and moony eyes, but she was a drug dealer—heroin. When she was caught, my mom lost her job and my dad's business went south." He spit. "What I'm saying is, I think you need to check up on that woman. She

112

and Rooster," he said vehemently, "could have been in cahoots with selling pot."

Although instinct told me his reasoning was clouded by emotion, of course I would run a check on the woman. "An excellent deduction," I said. "I'll do that."

Gator walked over to a clump of thick bamboo, turned his back to me, unzipped his pants and peed. I looked away.

Later, I dropped him off on May Street and went straight to my room. The day had taken its toll, especially the whole Kennedy cosmic or sexual whatever thing which had caused me so much confusion. Thoughts of Ku Klux Klan activities and drug dealing didn't help either.

19

I opened the fridge and grabbed a bottle of water and then stretched out on the bed. I missed Gar. More than . . . Well, I just missed him.

I picked up my iPad and googled Bev Seagate. She had lived in her home for over forty years, had been married to a man for thirty years who had died two years ago of a heart attack. She'd been a secretary at a realty office in Punta Gorda for the last ten years. No police record. No DUIs. No reason to think she was a drug pusher or killer, but then such bare facts never really imparted much information about what really went on in a person's life. She'd been a friend of Rooster's. She could have been a partner in crime. People were often killed by those close to them.

Next I typed in "Benjamin Clipp" according to the list Kennedy gave me—aka T-Strap. He had been arrested twice for misdemeanors. Served six months in a juvenile home.

Samuel Kennedy was married—wife Sarah. No kids. No debts. No DUIs or arrests. A pastor for fifteen years. Before that he was a co-owner of a junkyard. Lived in Punta Gorda.

Eleanor George, an active volunteer and philanthropist her whole life, had never worked outside the home. Married to Charles George (attorney) for sixty years. Went blind after a car accident more than twenty years ago during the move from Mississippi to Florida. Car ran her off the road. Driver of car never found. No DUIs. No arrests. No debts.

Unable to find out if Jonah Henning had any connection with the Klan, I decided I would call my trusty old boss later

114

(when I knew he would be available to take the call) to help me on that score.

I opened the "Rooster" folder on my iPad and added the information I'd learned, including the names of the people who had blackballed him. I copied the names of the men beside Stoner that he played poker with: Scotty Faulkner, Tom Chase, and Eddie Crone. Then I made separate folders for Sadi, Eleanor George and her husband, the pastor, T-Strap, Bev Seagate, and each of the others I had yet to interview. I set down my iPad and started to stand, sat and picked it up again and typed in a reminder to also talk to the principal of the middle school Rooster had worked at. I hesitated, there was another reminder I needed to add, but it didn't come to me. Knowing it would eventually, I closed the iPad.

To my delight, I spent the afternoon sketching the sanctuary of the church and different angles of Kennedy and T-Strap's profiles. In one of the sketches Kennedy's face filled the page. His hand rested on the head of T-Strap.

Thrilled with my creative accomplishment, I jumped off the bed, switched on the radio and began gyrating my hips, pumping my hands, moving my bare feet. Who cared that I could never find the beat? Who cared that my loosened hair flopped back and forth like a mop?

Sweat beads dotted my forehead. My breath came in gasps. I dropped onto the bed and watched the ceiling fan whirl. Grandma Murphy would have called that spontaneous victory dance a Jessie Moment. Mom would have said such bizarre behavior proved my incompetence. The fan blades looked like an airplane propeller. I raised my hands and gazed at my fingers. I'd had far too few Jessie Moments these past months—far too few.

115

Clearing my throat, I called Hawk and asked him to check if Jonah Henning's name had ever been connected with the Klan in Neshoba County, Mississippi. When I gave him the name that I had copied from the photo of Sam Bowers Jr, he whistled. I think I know that name," he said. "If I'm right, he was the Imperial Wizard of the Klan in that area."

"Really!"

"Don't jump to conclusions. I need to check that I'm right. I'll get back to you." He warned me to be careful before he hung up. "The Klan is not dead, Jessie. Not by a long shot."

I had only interviewed a few people at this point, but I made a suspect list anyway:

1. Sadi's boyfriend, Jack Lesan. Motive: Jealousy.

2. Bev Seagate. Motive: In cahoots with Rooster (maybe a pot connection), afraid her cover would be blown.

3. T-Strap. Motive: Perhaps got pissed off when Rooster wouldn't sell him pot. Or, Rooster was selling him pot and something went wrong enough to piss T-Strap off.

4. Samuel Kennedy. Motive: Found out about Rooster selling the kids of his congregation pot and in anger shot him.

5. The parents on the list. Motive: Thought he was an abuser.

6. Any kid he may have abused. Motive: Revenge.

7. Whoever he feared from his Klan past, if there was one—Motive: Revenge.

I began to close out the file, but then added one more name:

8. Stoner Taylor. Motive: Two possibilities: Rooster knew something about Stoner's past and he was going to talk. Or, Stoner killed Rooster in a fit of rage when he found out Rooster had lost the shipment of pot.

I had a strong feeling that Stoner was involved in the pot operation. Hiring me could just be a way of deflecting suspicion off himself.

A formidable gale blew across the water.

20

Tap. Tap. Tap.

Slowly and cautiously I raised one blind. I almost jumped out of my freckled skin when I saw Russ Beadle's rugged, bulldog face pressed against the glass, hand cupped over eyes. "Hey!" I yelped, dropping my pen. This was not a mug I wanted to see. Hunkering down, I grabbed my pen and carried it to the door with me, checking my phone for the time. Nine p.m.

"I thought you'd never answer," Beadle said. "I knocked on the door for a long time. You sleepin' again?"

I ignored his question. He pushed open the door and all but blew into my room. "Damn, what a night."

I glowered at him as I pushed the door open wide. I really didn't want him in my personal space, but here he was. Sometimes I couldn't win for losing. "Did I say you could come in? Get out!"

"There's a problem."

"Yeah?"

"Stoner's gone missin'."

"You're kidding, right?" First Zen, then Gar, now Stoner? What was wrong with this place?

"Gone missing? Or you can't locate him?" I asked.

"Missin', I said. Didn't I? No one's seen him since this morning. The bait shop's been closed all day. His wife is frantic."

"You called the cops?"

118

"Sure. But they got this twenty-four hour rule. Good God, what's the magic about twenty-four hours? Lots can happen in that amount of time. We got to search for him."

"We?"

"Listen, woman, you and I ain't buddies, that's no lie. But Stoner is out there somewhere needin' help. He hired you!" He withheld saying "bitch," but I heard it. Oh yes, I heard it.

I looked at him in frustration. "What can I do? I'm no missing person expert. I'm not even local. I wouldn't even know where to start."

Beadle collapsed onto the mattress. All his bravado went out of him. His body seemed to implode. His voice cracked as he spoke. But all I was thinking about was the disinfectant I was going to have to buy to spray on the bedspread.

"I don't know what to do either." He held his burly head in his hands.

I began to pace. "Okay, okay," I said as much to myself as to him. I stopped at the end of the bed. "Get up, will you? When was he last seen?"

He stood. "When he left for work this morning. No one saw him after that. I asked everyone and I mean everyone."

I paced some more. This had to have something to do with Rooster's murder. But what? All I'd found out about Rooster was that he lived in fear and tried to help young African-American kids which had caused him to be suspected of being a pedophile, that he was a possible former (or not former) Klan member, transferred pot from Colorado to Florida, and potentially he sold pot to those very same kids. Where did Stoner fit into the equation, other than being a close friend? They'd been school buddies since grade school in Mississippi. Sadi said they were as close as Robin and Superman. Did they both live in fear? Was Stoner's life in danger too? I grabbed my cap.

"Take me to Stoner's wife," I said.

Beadle's pickup made a dumpster look like an anal attentive lawyer's file cabinet. In an act of self-preservation from the caustic smells of foul food wrappers sticking out from a filthy white (I'm sure it was once white) five-gallon bucket, body sweat, stale tobacco, and fish and bait remains, I rolled my window down and pulled my body in tight as if that would keep me from getting rabies. The seat beneath me was torn from back to front. I readjusted my rear so I wouldn't get cut.

I slammed my flip flops on the dashboard as the pickup shot out of the parking space like a gigantean striking croc.

21

An anxious-faced young woman answered the door on the first knock.

We ignored the usual introductions and got right down to business, sitting at the kitchen table. She knew who I was and said so. I wasted no time getting down to specifics.

"Did your husband seem different when he left this morning? Did anything seem odd?"

"Not really. Oh, he was sadder `cause of Rooster, but he was glad you had agreed to help find the ki . . ." Her words faded away.

"I keep hearing from people that Rooster lived in fear. What about Stoner?"

Her gaze shot like a pinball around the room, landed on Beadle then lowered. Her voice was a murmur. "He has nightmares. But Jesus saves. I keep telling him that."

"Uh, yes, of course. But what were the nightmares about?"

"About?"

I nodded.

"Oh, trains running over his head, ghouls gnawing at his eyes. Things like that. I told him they were the devil's working. I told him if he'd take Jesus as his savior they'd stop."

"So you don't think he was afraid of something?"

"Sure he was. That's what I said, didn't I? Nothin` is more real than the devil, `cept Jesus of course."

"Um, yes, but did you ever discuss his fears with him?" I asked.

She looked hard at Beadle. "What's discussing Stoner's personal life got to do with him leaving without a word? God won't like it if he knows I'm talkin` about my husband behind his back."

Beadle leaned forward ready to speak, but I spoke up first. "Mrs. Taylor, if you want us to search for your husband, we have to have some idea what we're searching for."

"God will provide," she said.

Exasperated, I caught Beadle's eye. He took over. "Lily, this gal's trying to help. I've been lots of places already, asked lots of questions, but no one seems to have seen Stoner after he left here. I'm sure God wants him safe. Has he ever disappeared like this before?"

Lily shook her head rigorously and burst into sobs.

Beadle and I exchanged glances, again neither of us spoke. After a few more awkward moments, I puffed out my cheeks and took her hand. "If you ever heard Stoner talk about a certain person or persons who might have it in for him, now is the time to tell us."

Lily sniffled. "I wish I had, but Stoner, he wasn't one for sharin`. You know men, they don't talk much. Not like women, are they?" She blew her nose with a paper napkin.

I leaned back in my chair. Scratched around in my gray matter. Wished I was smarter and more experienced than I was. "Mind if I look around?"

She didn't. I stood. Beadle assured Lily that we would find Stoner. I wished I had his confidence. I roamed the room, having no idea what I was looking for. I went into the bedroom and stopped dead still. Hanging over the bed was another copy of the print that Rooster owned, the one with an

122

African-American woman sitting on the front seat of a bus. Again, I wondered what a white guy, now two white guys who had gone to school together in Mississippi were doing with such a print. In fact, the same one. Were they sympathetic to integration or hostile toward it?

When I asked Lily about it, she said almost the same thing that Sadi had said, "It was the one thing he owned that meant a lot to him."

Hmm.

I sat again with Beadle and Lily whose tears had subsided. I was prepared to tell her that we had to wait until morning to start any search. "I think we have to . . ."

The loud bang of car doors slamming, of tires cracking gravel, of raised voices, and of click of metal against metal, broke into my words. I shot a glance at Beadle. He stood and now looked like a giant Sasquatch from the wild in the tiny kitchen with the seven-foot ceiling and yellow curtains.

"They're here," he said taking long strides to the door.

"They?" I followed him out into the damp night where at least a dozen men and women had gathered, some holding rifles, others shotguns. I scanned the crowd. No Gator. No Zen. No cops. Gator's absence surprised me. Not Zen's. Definitely not the cops.

"What's this all about?" I asked in a harsh whisper. Why I was suddenly whispering I had no idea. Or was it that seeing this posse (because that is definitely what it looked like) made me think I had just stepped into a western and had to be quiet on the set.

"I called them before I came to you. We're not setting around until mornin`." He looked at me. "You with us?"

Normally I don't allow a man, any man, even Hawk, to make my investigative decisions for me, especially ones that

I thought were totally bogus. But it was obvious that if I refused to help in this search, I would lose all credibility and trust I had built up with the locals. Thus, I had no choice. Another position I hated to be in. I nodded.

I held back while Beadle divided everyone into groups of two, giving them particular areas to search on Pine Island and in Matlacha. My partner, a guy named Noodle who was tall, skinny, pock-marked, and flat-nosed, said he was "packin'". Luckily he kept his gun concealed. He and I were to take the Waterfront Restaurant and houses and vacant lots in St. James City proper.

Spending the night with a guy named Noodle in a search that I believed futile put me into a dark and steely mood that resembled my Grandma Murphy's on the day she was told that she should no longer drive. Not that she had stopped driving. "What will they do, arrest me?" she'd said in a threatening voice that made her terrier scurry under the sofa and not come out for half a day.

I had no doubt the whole plan was pointless. There were too many buildings and vacant lots, many of them isolated, to hide a body or a kidnap victim. Too much mangrove. Too many deserted tree farms. And there were multiple boats in yards or stored on lifts. But Beadle would not listen. Stoner was the man who provided them bait to fish. He was one of them. They had to do something. I was glad to see Beadle climb back into his truck with the bleached-blonde masseuse who had a Glock in a black leather holder visible under her gauzy shirt. Wasn't she the one Jay Mann was seeing? I wondered if Jay knew she carried a gun. The thought of him discovering a gun under her nightie almost made me laugh. But I caught myself in time. Wrong time. Wrong place. Wrong picture to paint.

With my mood slightly shifted toward the lighter side of things, I opened the door to Noodle's truck and hopped in. "You keep that gun hidden, hear me?" I warned.

He shrugged. "I had my trainin`. Don't worry."

"Keep it holstered," I shot back.

Noodle raised his eyebrows and gave me a long look, opened his mustache-covered mouth then clamped it shut. Guess my red hair and the extinguisher in my eyes put out his fire.

The Waterfront had their closed sign out. The door was locked. Noodle tapped on the window. An overly made up young waitress who had the same helpful disgruntled attitude as an airline attendant opened the door a crack and said, "Can't you see we're closed?" and started to shut it. But before she succeeded, I slipped in my flip flop clad foot and told her our mission. Her attitude did a one hundred and eighty degree shift. Now concerned and very much wanting to help, she said she hadn't seen Stoner, but we could talk to the manager who was out back.

The night was steamy; the wind had died out. We walked through air that was like sweat on a glass filled with ice, slippery and illusive. At the foot of the steps, a muscle-bound man stood on one leg, the other pressed against a piling, his face expressionless and solid like a carved image on a log. We passed him, making sure not to touch him, and he didn't blink an eye, but he knew we were there and we knew he knew we were there. I once knew a bouncer in Boston and he was like this guy—on the tad scary side, but harmless enough if you kept your nose clean on his watch.

The back dock was big enough for a single line of narrow roughhewn tables. A woman sat at the far end concentrating on a stack of receipts, facing several pricey houses lining the shore across the water. Boats were bedded for the night on lifts or tied to pilings. The channel gurgled and swayed. A white egret stood on the bow of a sailboat, head raised, poised and regal.

I walked to the woman. She looked bored, definitely bored, but busy. Noodle remained near the closed door. The woman didn't look up when she asked, "What can I do for you?"

I repeated our purpose.

"Damn, he went missing? Lily has to be frantic. Men? He comes around. Stays too long. Drinks too much. Haven't seen him today, though."

She stood and walked to the door, unlocked it and motioned us in. "Ask, Sal if she's seen him. Tell Lily she has our prayers."

The restaurant looked like an abandoned adult play school. It smelled of fried food and disinfectant. Both odors seemed to emanate from the kids' colored drawings that plastered the walls and hung down from the ceiling beams. Near the cash register, a bottle of ale gleamed like a sailor's glass eye. We scanned the empty dining area then went into the bar where two men were finishing their drinks. I headed for the kitchen. Noodle took the storage room. The waitress, who I assumed was Sal, said nothing as she watched, standing under a sign that announced: *If You're Going to Be a Turd Go Lay in the Yard*. Couldn't help but wonder where Beadle's spot was in the grass. T-shirts were folded and nailed or tacked to the ceiling. A bulletin board was filled with fishing photos.

The customers stood.

"Bye guys, thanks so very much," the waitress said. "Don't forget now, Thursday's special is little necks."

I went to the bar.

126

"Having any luck, dear? I wish I could help you more."

"Who else worked here today?"

"Oh, Bet and the cook. They've already gone home. Wish I could call them for you, I really do, but they don't have phones. In fact, dear, none of us here know where they live."

There's something about being called "dear" by a woman my same age that bugs me. Call me a word snob, but really! I shook my head.

Convinced Stoner was nowhere on the premises, we left. I said I'd take the southernmost three streets and Noodle could take the next three and we'd continue in that pattern until we'd done this end of St. James City on foot. That way we wouldn't be that far apart as we scoured the area. If one of us needed the other, we wouldn't be apart. We both had cell phones, so communication was easy. Once this was done, we'd get back into his truck and scope out the remainder of the town.

I gave myself a wide berth around a large dumpster obliterating the front door of the inn. This whole bogus search was making me grumpier by the minute. I should be in my room. Dumpsters, especially open ones, were one of my pet peeves. Like BIG TIME! Windows, kitchen cabinets, various sized boards, and sheetrock stuck out haphazardly from the open metal monster. A smell like rotting sea bass permeated the contents. Eww. I stepped around it. Tripped over an outstretched . . .

"Noodle!" I screamed at my phone. "Get back to the Waterfront!"

Stoner was propped up against the dumpster, his head leaned against his left shoulder. His legs were splayed out in front of his body reminding me of a chicken's wishbone before it was cracked. My bare toe had caught the edge of his jeans.

Hesitantly, not wanting to find out he was dead, I closed my eyes, gauging how long it would take Noodle to get here. When I heard his footsteps coming close, I hunkered down and put my ear near Stoner's chest, then recoiled.

"Is he . . . ?"

22

The next day I slept until noon. By the time we had hauled the drunken Stoner home and settled him into his praying wife's arms and made phone calls and arrived back to my room, it was 4 a.m. I'm not a 4 a.m. kind of gal.

It was 1 p.m. when I began my power walk. The sun was high in the sky and it was as hot as an overheated porcelain plate in a microwave, but welcomed. I wanted more than anything to sweat off any residuals of last night: being in Russ's truck, searching premises with an armed guy named Noodle, my feelings of horror at the shock of thinking I'd found a dead man. I raised my closed fists high as I pumped, shooting through the community park pretending I was an avenging shark after prey.

My plan today was to talk to Stoner. Get the lowdown on his past with Rooster. Convince him that I couldn't operate without knowing the full truth. I slowed my pace, cooling down. Then raising my arms above my head, I continued around the park. Out of breath again, I sat on the bench in front of the beach (that-wasn't-a-beach). The stone I'd named Odessa because she resembled the goddess hadn't been moved. I released my backpack from my shoulder and took out a bottle of water and gulped several long swigs.

"Thought that was you," Gator said, as he approached from behind. Cut-offs, plastic flip flops, no shirt. Very Gator. I swear he'd sprayed himself with Chanel No. 5 home-brewed skunk perfume.

"I was planning to call you. I slept in," I said.

"I heard you had quite a night."

"Hmm."

"The whole town is talkin` about it. Hell, both islands are talkin` about it. You're a hero, girl."

"What?"

"Oh, yeah. Word has it you organized a posse and went out to find Stoner and found your man. People are more than impressed."

I shook my head and took another drink. "I didn't organize the posse."

"According to Stoner's wife and Beadle, you did."

"Humph!" I wondered what had gotten into Russ Beadle, making me out the leader and all. Must want something from me. Yeah, right! "I'm going to take a shower and then go talk to Stoner. Can you be ready in an hour?"

"Sure."

"Oh, and don't *you* forget to shower."

"Hey! I just did."

Great. Just great.

We left in one hour on the dot. I cautioned Gator not to mention the hood. We would keep that find to ourselves for the time being. He warned me that Stoner wouldn't be much up for talking. "Like duh!" was what I said. I meant, REALLY! MEN!!

Stoner was sprawled out on the ratty sofa but untangled his body from its prone position to sit when we walked in the door. Neither Lily nor the kids were around. Stoner ran his hand through his disheveled hair and looked at us through lowered eyelids. The whites of his eyes were bloodshot and his pupils were dilated. I was amazed he could see. He was wearing the same clothes he'd had on last night and needed a shave. The windows were open. I went back and secured the door so air could come in, then I sat beside Gator.

"Thanks for hauling my ass home," Stoner grumbled, jiggling his head as if he had a tic in his ear.

"You get plastered often?" I asked.

"Been quite a spell. Lily don't approve. Says I'll rot in Hell. Guess Rooster's death has me goin`. Guess The Hell Threat didn't work this time. Have any luck finding the killer?"

"Not yet. But I need your help."

He eyed me with a curious, low-eyelid expression.

"Rooster, you said, lived in fear. How about you?"

"God, my head." He stood, stumbled to the sink and filled a glass from the tap and set it on the countertop. Unscrewing the lid from a medicine bottle, he popped two pills, following them with several gulps of water. He leaned toward the window. "Looks like a good day for fishin`. Hope Lily got the shop open for the early crowd."

"She did," Gator said.

Stoner smiled crookedly at Gator. "Not much of a livin` selling bait, but it pays the bills." He walked back to the sofa and fell onto it with a groan. I wondered how long he planned to stall, or was he buying time to come up with a good story? Or was he just working on his male bonding skills with my partner?

"Do you live in fear?" I repeated.

He looked me directly in the eye. "Nope, not me, not Stoner," he said, not blinking.

"You know I can't be of much good if people aren't honest with me. You know that, right?"

"Imagine that's true. But as I said, Rooster had something or someone chasing after him, I don't . . . but as I think on it I

131

can see why you might come to that conclusion, what with me and Roost's close friendship and all."

Uh, huh! Fabricated story down pat. I switched gears.

"When I was here the other day I happened to notice you had a print in your bedroom that was the same as one Rooster owned. That seemed odd to me. What's the story there?"

Stoner rubbed his head again. "Oh, that. Our folks got together and gave us those. Said it would remind us of what was right and what was wrong. I'm sure you know the subject matter—Rosa Parks on the bus?"

"And what did your folks think was right and what wrong?"

"Never asked," he mumbled, then groaned and closed his eyes. He refused to answer any other questions. When Gator and I left, he was snoring.

I sat in the car while Gator leaned against it and had a cigarette. When he was done, he climbed inside.

As I turned the key in the ignition, the rear window exploded and Gator and I ducked. Terrified, we remained hunched over, gazing at each other.

"Your stalker?" Gator asked in a growly whisper.

I shook my head rigorously. "Rooster's killer."

"Coward!" Gator hissed.

We remained hunkered down until my door snapped open and Stoner, holding a shotgun, gazed at us. "I think he's gone. Did you see him?" he asked.

"No, let's get inside," I said in a hushed voice, "no telling where he is. Stay down."

Tumbling out of the car, we bent low at the waist and made it back to the house. We rushed inside, slammed the door and secured the chain lock. "Stay lower than the windows." I said, tapping in 911. We eyed each other as I gushed out our need for help.

"Blast it to hell," Gator growled at Stoner, "You're too drunk to handle that shotgun, toss it over!" He glanced toward me. "Excuse the French."

An owl hooted.

A twig snapped.

23

Abrupt, rapid pounding rattled the flimsy door. "Hey, in there. It's Tobin Peterson. Open up."

Relieved, I pushed up from the floor. Releasing the chain lock, I opened the door. "What took you so long?" I asked, surprised my voice came out so strong.

"You okay?" Stepping inside, Tobin and two deputies took in the room: Me looking, I'm sure, frazzled. Gator holding the shotgun, Stoner squeezed against the wall under the window. "What happened here?"

In rapid word fire, I filled him in.

"Okay, stay out of sight. John, you stay outside near the door. Ali, you and I'll search the area." He looked at me. "Bolt the door."

"Be careful," I whispered, securing the latch. Settling again on the floor, I distracted myself by giving my attention to a pair of dolls to my right. A matched set. Twins. A gift card hung from the wrist of the closest one. *To Faith, Love Uncle Rooster.*

"They're not going to find anyone," Stoner said. "Anyone sees a squad car and they'd take off."

The doorknob turned. I blanched.

"It's us. Open up," Tobin shouted.

Gator shot up, hurried to the door and unlatched it.

"Put the shotgun down," Tobin said. "We're much safer when you're holding a fishing pole."

"You got that right," Gator said, leaning the gun against the table. "See anything?"

134

"Nah. Whoever it was is long gone. But we found a couple of bullet shells. We'll have them checked. That will at least let us know what kind of weapon was used."

Tobin questioned each of us, taking down our accounts. We left my car parked so it could be gone over by the cops. One cop took Gator and me back to Matlacha. Stoner said he and his family would spend the night with neighbors. Gator slithered to Bert's for a beer. I hightailed it to my room to get my iPad, switching on the Internet. The first thing I typed in was "Rosa Parks."

I spent the next couple of hours surfing the web, taking notes, thinking. Tobin, no longer dressed in his cop uniform, showed up around eight. I was more than glad to see him.

He told me he had heard I'd joined the posse, said it was a reckless thing to do. I couldn't disagree with him, but I was excited about what I'd learned.

I turned the conversation to my research. Everything seemed to confirm my suspicions about involvement in the Klan. "Stoner was a high school senior at Neshoba County High School the year over seven hundred college students from across the states descended on Mississippi to register African-Americans to vote, did you know that?"

"Yeah, but that doesn't prove anything. Stoner could have been for segregation, not against it."

"Yeah, of course, but Gator found a Klan hood at Rooster's home. Why would he have that?"

I could tell I'd gotten Tobin's attention. I continued, "The Klan went crazy that summer. You may already know this, but I didn't. The first day the Freedom Riders arrived three volunteers went missing. They were later found murdered. The sheriff and deputy, amongst other Klan members were later convicted. But floggings, church burnings, other deaths. They were all part of that lawless time."

"This isn't news to me, Jessie. The Florida Klan was pretty active back then too. My grandparents were de-segregationists. Their lives were threatened more than once." His expression went more solemn. "Are you sure it was a Klan hood?"

I stood, went to my nightstand and pulled open the drawer. Withdrew it. Held it up.

"Yep, that's a Klan hood all right. I'm surprised Sadi gave it to you."

My face reddened.

"You stole it?"

"Well, it wasn't actually me."

"Okay, just put it away. I didn't see it. It could never be used as evidence."

"Even if it's returned?"

"I didn't hear that."

I replaced the hood in its hiding place, then went back and sat on the chair, placing my hands on the table.

"So," he said, "tell me your theory."

"I think it's highly possible that Stoner and Rooster were Klan members and took part in some unspeakable act that summer. Since then, it's probable they've both lived in fear of retribution. They left Mississippi because they were known there. Rooster may have attemped to make restitution by doing what he could to help teen African-Americans at his church. But someone found out who he was and killed him. That same someone could now be after Stoner."

"This is all speculation, right?"

I slumped back into my chair. "True."

He reached across the table and took my hands in his. Although his action made me feel uncomfortable, I didn't pull away. He had on that frayed shirt that endeared me to him. "Until you do, I'd keep that theory to yourself. Nothing good would come from you spreading conjecture."

Tobin was right. Without proof, the theory was just that— instinct-driven supposition. One thing a PI had to do was to not jump to conclusions too early in the investigation. Doing that could stall progress for several months. I had lots more people to question. Who knew? Maybe another lead would uncover completely different information leading to a whole new set of conclusions. And, of course, my theory ignored the child abuse accusations. What would a parent do if they discovered a trusted adult was sexually abusing their kid? What might a kid do if he were being abused? And why target Stoner?

Another part of my suspicious brain boiled and bubbled with a troubling question: Why *really* did Tobin want me to keep the speculation to myself?

Tobin squeezed my hands. I nodded my answer while deciding to keep the abuse accusation information between Gator and me. It was a far-fetched idea. Much more far-fetched than my current theory.

"I'm worried about you," he said. "I want you . . . to stay safe."

My cheeks reddened. I looked at his large hands that covered mine and smiled thinly.

Very thinly.

24

I bounced out of bed determined to track down the killer who I was sure had shot at us. Another unpleasant thought struck me. Would my car insurance cover the replacement of a window that had been shot out? I had five-hundred dollar deductible. At the very least, that amount would have to be tacked onto my invoice for Stoner. After all, the damage was caused while I was on the job.

I showered, dried my hair and slithered into my sport shorts, T-shirt, and tennis shoes, going over what had happened the night before:

Talked to Stoner. Returned to car with Gator. Gator had a smoke. Got in car. Sat talking for a while. Shot at. Stoner arrived, shotgun in hand. Rushed back into house. Called cops. Tobin and two deputies arrived in separate cruisers.

Some detail was eluding me. But whatever it was wouldn't come to the surface. I let the idea go for the time being.

Since I'd not heard back from Hawk about possible Klan involvement or for that matter any other information about Rooster, I knew it was time to broaden my investigation. I opened my iPad and perused my notes. I'd start with Sadi's ex-boyfriend. See where that led me.

It didn't take me long to discover Jack Lesan lived in Matlacha. When I phoned his number, he answered on the second ring, but he was on his boat, fishing. He'd be back in around 10 and would be happy to talk to me then. He gave me his address (which I already had) and I hung up and immediately phoned Gator. I left a message on his voicemail.

Satisfied with my plan, I snatched up my cap and headed out the door for my walk. The sea was calm and dotted with several anchored fishing boats. Pelicans soared and nose-dived. Traffic rumbled over the bridge. A line of kayakers paddled toward a distant mangrove island. A crabber tugged in a trap and emptied it with a flourish. The parking lot in the park was filled with pickups and their attached boat trailers. A white egret strolled regally toward the fishing dock.

As usual, I kept up a steady, high arm pumping pace. I couldn't believe how hungry I was. Instead of my normal breakfast bar, I decided to go to The Perfect Cup.

The café was packed as usual with locals and tourists. I weaved through the crowd. Nodded at friendly faces. Exchanged an occasional hello.

"That's her," I heard a woman whisper.

I frowned, but then remembered that some of these people were under the mistaken impression that it was me who organized the posse to search for Stoner. Since I was sweaty from my walk, I wondered what they thought of the image I projected. Did it match their idea of what a heroine should look like? I grinned inwardly when Wonder Woman came to mind. Wonder Woman I wasn't. More like Pippi Longstocking.

Zen was sitting alone at a table in the back room. After getting a cup of coffee, I headed her way.

"Hey!" I said.

Zen's smile was contagious.

I sat and she began to talk so fast I finally raised my hand to slow her down.

She laughed. "Oh, hon, I'm just so in love. I can't help myself. He's such a good man. I'm the luckiest girl in the world." She glanced at the wall clock, apologized and stood. "He's expecting me in five." She leaned down and hugged me. "So great to see you. Bye."

I shook my head, hoping this was the one for Zen. I looked around. No Gator.

The waitress came to the table and I ordered a full breakfast, eggs over easy, bacon, and muffin. Jay Mann, the sculptor and my former brief fling, passed the waitress, coffee mug in hand. "Hey, girl, you haven't stopped in. Should I feel insulted?"

"I've been crazy busy. Join me."

He sat. "Uh, this job for Stoner…" He hesitated.

"Yeah?"

"Stoner isn't my favorite guy. Be cautious with him. He's, uh, more than he appears."

I was all ears. "Details, please," I said, leaning toward him.

Jay glanced around, then shook his head. The waitress was coming our way. He lowered his voice. "Just be careful," he said, then excused himself and left.

It wasn't like Jay to be so mysterious, so secretive. I would have to pin him down. But his words confirmed my earlier suspicions about Stoner. I hoped Hawk would get to me sooner rather than later. I was sure that anything he discovered about Rooster would somehow connect to his bud, Stoner.

After finishing my meal, I rushed back to my room to shower. By 9:45 I still hadn't heard from Gator, so I decided to walk to Jack Lesan's alone. A woman in a straw hat on a bicycle pedaled past and smiled. An osprey's cuk cuk and the growl of traffic crossing the bridge were the most prominent sounds I heard as I headed down Island Ave.

Lesan lived on Geary Street. The house was a three-story number, one of those million-dollar water view wonders. An SUV that had to be sixty grand easy filled one side of the parking space in front of the garage. I found him on the back dock cleaning fish. Two white cranes strolled around the sparse yard. Four brown pelicans circled a pricey Tiara. This was a guy who had money. No doubt about that. Lesan had on shorts and a white T-shirt. He appeared to be in his mid-forties and was movie-star handsome. I thought of Sadi and her now damaged looks and felt an even deeper empathy for her.

Lesan's greeting was friendly, but his attention remained on the pile of fish on the wooden table and the knife in his hand. He cut off a head with one quick motion then threw it high into the air. The pelicans' mouths opened as they swam into position. The head descended, landing in the bill of the pelican farthest from the boat. Lesan chuckled and continued his work.

"What kind of fish are they?"

"Sea bass." He tossed another head. It landed in the Tiara. A pelican hopped to the edge, ducked its head and snatched it up. "Sadi said you'd be calling me."

"So you two are still friends?"

"Sure. Why wouldn't we be?"

"I suppose she told you that I'm looking into Rooster's death?"

"Yep. And you're wondering if me and Rooster hated each other. No way. Rooster was like me. A live and let live kind of guy. Sharing women don't ruffle our feathers."

"Quite a philosophy," I said.

He shrugged. "Makes life easier and most definitely more fun. Right now I'm dating two bisexuals." He sliced a fish down the center of its belly and drew out the guts with the tip of the knife. "Sorry to disappoint you. Me and Rooster actually appreciated each other," he said, tossing the entrails into the water. "Had lots in common, if you know what I mean. I didn't know Rooster well. He wasn't one to talk much about himself. If you want to know more about him, talk to his poker buddies."

"Just one more question."

"Yeah."

"Where were you the night Rooster was shot?"

He smiled and shook his knife at me. "Persistent thing, aren't you?" He looked me up and down. "I like that quality in a gal."

I said nothing.

He picked up another bass. "As a matter of fact I was with Sadi. She called me. She was real upset. I stayed with her a couple of days to help with the kids. She gets real down sometimes."

"There's one thing I wonder about."

"Yeah, what?"

I swept my hand around his house, his property. "You have so much. I'm surprised you didn't help Sadi with her bills. They had to be fearsome."

"Who said I didn't? Think I'm a scumbag or something? I handed Rooster a check a couple of weeks ago. It was cashed the next day. The amount should have easily covered her recent medical bills." He cut off another head.

I was puzzled. Of course, there was no reason Sadi should have offered this information and I certainly had not brought up her financial situation. According to Hawk's research, Sadi was still recovering from the deep wounds of hospital and doctor bills. So, what had Rooster done with the money? And hadn't his sister also said she paid those bills? Seemed Rooster had been working the "poor Sadi" angle from both ends of a candle. Apparently, the story he told his yoga teacher was a lie too. He certainly didn't need to haul a van of marijuana to come to his ex-wife's financial rescue. Rooster was indeed quite the poker player. Most likely a poorly played hand had gotten him killed.

Lesan brought me out of my reverie when he stuck his eight-inch knife blade deep into the wood of the cutting table. I watched it quiver, said my farewell and began to retrace my steps.

"Hey!"

I stopped and looked over my shoulder.

"Wanta get a drink some time?"

I flipped my ponytail at him and walked away.

Lesan's laughter was louder than the overhead osprey's mating call. I made a mental note to find out where Lesan got his money.

25

I took the chance that Rooster's poker buddy, Scotty Faulkner, would be home. He lived on the next canal over from Lesan. He was tending his yard in front of his modest home, clipping off the tiny lavender flowers of the green stuff that covered the sandy soil. Real grass was sparse on the island. Many, especially snowbirds who wanted little lawn care, covered their lawns with rock. It didn't take them long to find out if you planted trees and scrubs, they could be higher than your roof in one season or if you weren't lucky, they could remain the same size forever, never growing. Faulkner must have a green thumb. His landscape was lush—something out of a magazine.

His shirt was drenched with sweat. I introduced myself and he invited me into the lanai for an ice tea.

"You have one of the most beautiful yards on this canal," I said.

"Yeah, well, lots of work. Sometimes it seems worth it." He set down two glasses. "I hope you don't use sugar. I don't keep any in the house."

"Don't, thanks."

A houseboat motored past. Faulkner waved. The occupants of the boat did too. I raised my glass.

"Hard to beat this," I said.

"Yeah. I used to live on Sanibel, but this life fits me better. I suppose you're here because of Rooster?"

"I am. I'm trying to get a full picture of his life, hoping some detail will be a clue to finding his killer."

"Figured. The poor sucker. Makes me sick to think of him no longer on this planet. He was one of the good ones."

"Anything you can tell me that would give me insight into his personality and private life could help."

"Damn excellent poker player. Never could read his face. A lot smarter than he liked to project. And sadder."

"Sadder?"

"Yeah, he shared something with me one night before the other guys got here, something that apparently ate at him quite a bit." He looked at me. "I told him I would keep his secret to myself, but well, now that he's dead . . . well . . . who knows? It might help you."

He took a drink then set down his glass. "He had a black mother. Now, in this day and age, not such a big deal anymore. Hell, plenty Americans are half something or other or gay or bi or even transsexual. I talked to him more than once about it, but he just clammed up and said to quit talking about it, said he was sorry that he'd ever confided in me. Said he sure didn't want Stoner to know. He was damn adamant." He sighed. "I guess I wasn't much help. I could tell it ate at him."

"I was told by his ex-wife and by Stoner that he was afraid of something."

"Yeah, he was afraid, but he would never talk about it and I mean, never. Whoever he was afraid of had him by the balls." He ducked his head. "Sorry."

"No problem. I get the picture."

"From what he said, his father hated him. His mother died at his birth. He was raised by a black nanny as if he were white."

"Did he ever mention his sister?"

"He did. He was real attached to her, but her husband hated him, especially when he found out he had black blood."

I recalled the husband's angry comment about Rooster just before they'd left the house, how Rooster had been a thorn in his wife's side. I guess if you were a bigot, that's what you'd think. Could he be a suspect? Maybe. All I knew about him was that he was a lawyer and a long-time husband to Rooster's sister. I made a mental note to add further facts to that data.

In the distance, Lesan's Tiara motored out.

"Do you know Jack Lesan?" I asked.

"Sure. Small island."

"Got any idea how he made his money?"

Faulkner chuckled. "That's a question often discussed at breakfast with the guys. No one seems to know."

Shortly after, giving him my cell phone number, I headed for my car. When I opened the door, Faulkner raised his hand to stop me. I waited. Faulkner hurried over.

"One thing I just thought of."

"Yeah."

"Odd thing. Maybe this won't help, but last time Rooster played poker you'd think he'd never played before. Didn't seem to know a flush from a four of a kind. The other guys and I talked about how he was off his game. We decided he was just distracted."

"When was that?"

"A week before he was murdered."

Sounded to me like Rooster's angst had reached a new height just before he was killed. Maybe the thought of hauling a van full of pot was the cause.

I left Scotty Faulkner convinced he wasn't involved in Rooster's death, but more than curious about Jack Lesan.

Only steps away I came upon a pelican perched on a mailbox. I hesitated. "Hi guy, how's things?"

The bird turned its head and stared directly into my eyes.

My hand went to my heart. "Will?" I whispered. "Is that you?"

The pelican raised and lowered its wings.

"Are you okay?" I asked, stepping forward.

The bird blinked, ducked its beak, opened its wings and flew away.

"Hey, that bird's name isn't Will," a man in the yard said.

"No, of course it isn't."

26

The following morning Gator and I talked with Tom Chase and Eddie Crone, the two other poker buddies. Neither of them had anything new to add to Faulkner's story. Neither said they knew any secrets about Rooster. Both said Rooster was a damn good poker player, except for the last night they'd played together.

At 1 p.m. we had an appointment with Roger and Sheila Turnstone, the parents of fifteen-year-old Tim. Roger said in our phone conversation that he had the day off from installing kitchen cabinets at a new housing development in the Cape. The cabinets had not come in. Sheila was taking off a day from her job as a social worker at an elderly care facility. They were hesitant to meet with us, but finally agreed. Jonah Henning was dead, Roger said, he was no longer a threat. I got the feeling they weren't too happy to help with finding his killer. But I could be wrong. I've been wrong before.

The Turnstones lived in a historic house a couple of blocks south of Punta Gorda Center. It was a two-story smallish Victorian surrounded by a picket fence. Vacant lots on either side of the house showed signs that once they had had neighbors. Most likely the houses had been damaged beyond repair by Hurricane Charley, a storm that had hit Punta Gorda with the force of a cigarette boat at full throttle.

A man in jeans and a red shirt stood at a side window, screen in hand. "Some day off," he said when he saw us. "Let's clean the windows, she insists. Whatever happened to: Let's go out to lunch and an art gallery?"

Gator closed and latched the gate as a woman in shorts and a sleeveless shirt stepped out the front door. She was carrying two bottles of what I assumed was window cleaner; a hefty stack of newspapers stuck out from under her left armpit. She smiled as we approached. "He complains, but he likes the windows clean more than I do." She set down the supplies and raised her voice. "Coffee's ready."

"Be right in. Just a sec," he called back.

It's not often in this part of Florida that I had the opportunity of going inside a Victorian home. Most homes are stucco over cement block constructions. This one was wood framed and had wood floors. Yellow pine, wide woodwork. The pungent smell of furniture polish told me what Sheila had just finished doing. I almost felt like I'd stepped back into my life in Cambridge, Mass. where these type of homes were as numerous as mallards on the Charles River.

We introduced ourselves, sized each other up and shook hands. Sheila was probably mid-forties and obviously worked out. She most likely wore a size six.

"You must be Ms. Murphy," Roger said as he gushed in the room, hand extended. I introduced Gator.

Roger chuckled. "Nice name. Only in the South," he said.

"Beats Nigel," Gator mumbled as he walked toward a large bird cage in the corner.

"Nigel?" I gasped, wishing I had kept my amazement to myself.

"Don't know what my folks were thinkin`," he said, sticking his finger in the cage. "Polly want a cracker?"

"Watch yourself. She bites," Sheila said. "Please, come into the living room."

Ignoring her warning, Gator continued to poke at the bird while talking to it.

I took the seat on the sofa that Sheila offered. Gator and the cage were in full view.

Roger asked how we liked our coffee.

"Black," I said.

"Got a Coke?" Gator yelled.

Sheila and I chatted about the house until Roger returned with a tray holding three mugs, a glass of Coke and a plate of cookies.

Gator spotted the cookies and hurried into the room. He snatched up three of the biggest ones before sitting. I gave him a "behave yourself" look. He winked at me, snatched up the glass of soda and slurped as he drank. I frowned and picked up the plate. "Here, have another one," I said, "I'm not hungry."

He grabbed a fourth one. I narrowed my eyes at him. He opened his mouth wide.

Roger and Sheila held hands as they watched our exchange. Hoping I could salvage some semblance of professionalism, I repeated the reason we were there, stressing that we were hired by Rooster's friend to help find his killer. Roger and Sheila nodded, but said nothing. The parrot in the cage squawked. Gator dropped a crumb on the floor and didn't bend to retrieve it. I scooped it up with my napkin and broke the awkward silence with a question.

"How old is your son?"

"Fifteen," they said in unison. Obviously they were anxious. I wished I'd had more experience in this type of interview. But this was my first to discuss possible child abuse with parents. And Gator was no help at all.

"We understand you were concerned about Jonah Henning's relationship with him?"

They looked at each other, then Roger leaned forward. "Our son was *not* and I repeat, *not* sexually abused. What we feared is that he might be."

"What caused you to fear such a thing?" I asked in a calm voice.

"A white man with two little kids of his own spending so much time with our teens. It wasn't right," Roger said.

"But surely there was something else that made you suspicious? Youth leaders usually have good intentions."

Roger squeezed his wife's hand and gave me a "Boy, are you naïve" look.

Sheila spoke up. "It was something Tim said." She clamped her mouth shut.

I looked from one to the other. I wanted to relieve them of their agony, but didn't know how. I glanced at Gator. He was nailing them with a fierce animal look. Oh, no!

I tried to get his attention, but I was too late. Gator was on the move. And when that happened, few humans could outrace him.

"Did he talk to them about sex?" Gator asked in his normal voice.

The couple squirmed.

"It wasn't right. Some white guy telling our son about condoms," Roger said.

"It just wasn't right," Sheila repeated in a voice so soft I barely heard her. "We prayed and prayed on it."

"That's a private subject between a boy and his folks. He had no right talking about such things. It was perverse."

"We took our complaint to Pastor Kennedy, but he wouldn't listen, so we called a meeting with the congregation," Sheila said.

"Ours wasn't the only complaint. Drug talk. Sex talk. The boys told their folks of course. He even told the boys he thought drugs should be legalized." Roger's voice had risen two octaves. He let go of his wife's hand. "Can you believe it?" The words were almost a shout.

Sheila patted her husband's shoulder and spoke in a soothing voice. "He had to go. There was no getting around it."

"But there was no evidence that Jonah had abused anyone, right?" I asked.

"Talk to the Kirkpatricks about that. They'll give you an earful," Roger said, still seething.

"As you know, Jonah was murdered," I said in an even voice.

Both of their expressions went blank.

I continued. "Okay, so you had a meeting. Jonah was asked to leave. Who delivered the message?"

"Mary Ellen," Sheila said.

I pulled a notebook from my breast pocket and scanned the names. "Mary Ellen Warner?"

"That's right. She volunteered. She said she wanted to see his face when she told him."

"Was there anyone at the meeting or that you talked to at all who seemed, well . . . seemed angrier than anyone else?"

"Do you mean was there anyone angry enough to kill him?" Roger asked.

"Yes."

"You're damn right there was. Every one of us. These are our kids. We're going to protect them, no matter what. The world is full of perverts." He shot out of his seat. "But not our kids. Not our kids!" His words vibrated around the room.

152

I gulped and was speechless. Gator, however, stood slowly. The men were the same height. "We get it," Gator said evenly. "Get it one hundred percent."

I don't know if it was the composure in Gator's voice or the words themselves, but Roger's anger defused as quickly as it had ignited. He seemed spent. Shook his head at any further questions. His wife, refusing to look at us, did the same. I left my phone number and we left.

Without me having asked all the questions I knew I should have, we stepped through their gate. Gator gave Roger, who stood in the doorway, a solemn salute before he latched it.

"Whew!" I said.

"A bomb ready to explode," he said, withdrawing his cigarette pack from his pocket.

We rounded the corner.

"Think he could kill?" I asked.

"To protect his young? Oh, yeah."

I thought so too.

We were to see Cheryl and Joe Kirkpatrick at 1:45. It was now 1:10. They were retired schoolteachers who had custody of their grandson. They also lived in Punta Gorda, but in a condo on Main Street.

Gator flicked his half-smoked cigarette into a potted hibiscus. I unlocked the car and recalled something else that had happened in the house. "Nigel, huh?"

"Our secret," he said.

"Just curious. What did you do before you came to Matlacha to fish?"

"Army sergeant."

"I can see that," I said.

His laughter was so loud I feared it made my dead grandpa turn over in his grave. But I'm sure he was smiling. He had been in the army too. Army took care of army. Oh, yes, Grandpa was smiling. That light in his eyes was new-penny bright. Just like whenever Grandma Murphy walked into a room.

27

Joe and Cheryl Kirkpatrick's condo was on the second floor. It was small, modern, and luxurious. Tan upholstered furniture. Oriental coffee table and end tables. Persian rug. Their balcony overlooked a restaurant and art gallery. Several pictures of a boy at various ages hung on one wall. I assumed it was their grandson Jake.

"Thanks for having us at such short notice," I said, shaking their hands.

Joe had snow-white hair and a wrinkle-free, pleasant dark-skinned face. He motioned for us to take chairs. "I'm glad we could accommodate you. This is the only free day we have. What with tennis, art classes, duplicate bridge, and our volunteer work, we're very busy. You said you wanted to speak to Jake. He'll be home shortly."

In a nervous gesture, Cheryl patted her strikingly beautiful silver hair. "We understand you came to talk about Jonah Henning. We were sorry to hear about, well, about his death." She seemed genuinely sorry.

"Yes, it was a terrible shame." I leaned forward. "If you don't mind, I'll get right to the point. We've been led to understand that you were part of a church group that accused Jonah of being a pedophile," I said. "Maybe or perhaps Roos . . . I mean, Jonah's death was somewhat of a relief?"

Joe reached for Cheryl's hand. "We are Christian people, Ms. Murphy. We get no pleasure in another's death. It is true Cheryl and I went to that meeting to decide what to do about him, but we were appalled at what they were saying. It seemed like a witch-hunt to us."

"You didn't believe he was a pedophile?" I asked.

Joe sat straighter in his chair. "Absolutely not. The man was willing to talk about issues other adults avoided with teens. We spent our lives teaching young people. We were thrilled that our grandson had Henning as a counselor."

"But . . ."

Joe did not wait for me to finish. "I understand your confusion. You came from the Turnstones. They knew we voted for Henning to be asked to leave, but they did not know why. They most likely assumed abuse was involved with our grandson. It was, but not like they thought. There are many types of abuse, all damaging." He hesitated.

Cheryl patted his hand and looked at me. "It was because of a different matter altogether. Our grandson is a football player and he's good. He's a senior in high school. Unfortunately, he's not college material. We have accepted that since he was in grade school."

Joe pulled his hand away.

"It's okay, hon. They need to know. Colleges were recruiting him. That's how good a player he is. He mentioned this to Henning who did the most amazing thing. The fact he did it and told us about it with no shame or remorse was totally unacceptable."

Gator was rigorously scratching what I assumed was a mosquito bite as he watched Joe.

"To get Jake's grade point raised from a 1.9, Henning signed him up for two online classes and took them for him. One night at a church meeting he casually and proudly told us about it. He said he got an A on the first test, so had to be careful after that. He made sure the rest of the grades were Bs.

He didn't want to make anyone suspicious. I guess he thought we would be pleased with him or some such rubbish. Instead, I expressed outrage. Henning was taken aback. I really don't think he thought what he had done was dishonest or wrong."

Cheryl's voice was low. "We hated what he had done. He was setting Jake up for failure. There is simply no way he should be going to college. And the dishonesty of the thing was disgusting. He wouldn't survive, not even with the best tutors. We were so embarrassed we never told the congregation why we were upset with Jonah. We are proud of our grandson. We pray that he will be a fine, honest, happy adult. Going to college is not for everyone."

Joe's expression was solemn. "Henning mocked everything we stand for. We were furious, but not so furious to want him dead."

I ended the questioning—more for a sense of closure and to satisfy Gator than anything else—by asking where they were the night Rooster was found. Football game then after party until 11. They readily supplied the names of two other couples who were with them all evening.

The front door opened and a tall, muscular teenager walked into the room.

"Jake, this is Ms. Murphy and . . ." Joe looked at Gator with a blank look on his face. I realized I'd failed to introduce him.

"Just call me Gator."

Joe smiled, but the smile was brief as he addressed his grandson. "They're investigating Jonah's death."

Jake sat and folded his hands in front of him. "Yeah. Glad someone is."

"We're trying to create a profile of Mr. Henning," I said. "Could you tell us what you thought of him?"

"Square guy." He glanced at his grandparents. "Guess it wasn't right for me to let him take those courses for me, but can't blame him. I'm the one who said go ahead. Rooster was only trying to help me."

"Of course he was," Cheryl said.

"My brain ain't so good as most," Jake added. Both grandparents protested.

"They (he nodded toward his grandparents) voted for him to be asked to leave. But it wasn't his fault and he wasn't interested in buggering boys either like those others thought. I ain't going back to that church again. Ever. Rooster lived by the Bible. He knew more Bible verses than any person I knew. He'd give you the shirt off his back. He was more Christian than anyone stepping into that church."

The Kirkpatricks hung their heads. Apparently this wasn't the first time their grandson had made this statement.

"When did you see him last?" Gator asked.

Jake's eyes narrowed. "At the stadium the night after he was asked to leave. He stopped in to say goodbye. Poor sucker. He had tears in his eyes. Shows what kind of a good man he was to show tears." He shifted away from Joe and Cheryl. Cheryl bit her lip. Joe shook his head and stared at the far wall.

"Sorry I have to ask this," Gator said, "but we got to cover our bases: Where were you the night he was killed?"

"Football game."

"They won," Mrs. Kirkpatrick chimed in, beaming.

Not long after, we left and I took the Kirkpatricks off the suspect list.

"That Rooster seems to have had plenty of cards up his sleeve," Gator said.

"Yeah, he was quite the game player."

28

Mary Ellen Warner worked for the state and was the single parent of a twelve-year-old boy. I made an appointment with her at 6 that night at which time, she said, her son would be at piano lessons. I would like to have met the son, but Mary Ellen seemed adverse to the idea and at this point there was nothing I could do about it.

In the meantime, I dropped off Gator at his place and spent the next couple of hours on my dock, sketching and contemplating the facts of the case. By the time I picked up Gator again, I had drawings of everyone we had interviewed, plus one of Jonah Henning, Stoner Taylor, and even Russ Beadle. I stacked them on the table near the window, waved to Gar and was on my way.

Mary Ellen lived in Fort Myers. We met at an open air restaurant on McGregor Boulevard.

Gator was dressed in jeans and a button-down plaid shirt that was only minimally frayed around the collar.

Mary Ellen and I ordered a glass of chardonnay, Gator a Corona.

Mary Ellen had a way of sitting up straight that made me think of Grandma. Her Afro created a halo around her head. Hoop earrings almost touched her red-striped blouse. On the back of her right wrist she had a tattoo of a small butterfly.

"Great tat," I said.

She grinned. "You should have heard my son after I got it. He was appalled. Moms don't get tattoos, he said. Guess I fooled him." She sobered. "You want to know what I told Jonah Henning, right?"

"I was wondering why you volunteered to pass on the news," I said.

"Like everyone else, I was upset, but I'm able to keep my emotions in check. Many at the meeting aren't. I figured if someone else told him there might be some physical confrontation. Someone might even get hurt. I didn't want that."

"I see."

"It wasn't easy to demand someone leave our congregation. I was also worried about getting sued for defamation of character, but it had to be done. I puzzled over it for some time. But when I talked to Jonah, he made it easy on me. I said my piece and he simply walked away. Didn't argue or anything."

Gator set his beer bottle on the table. "If ya'all thought he was a pedophile, why didn't you turn him in?"

"There was no proof. Plus, to be honest, I think everyone was really upset about what he talked to the kids about more than anything else. I really think that was why they wanted him to leave. The pedophile thing; that was, in my opinion, probably, well, most likely, a false accusation and most knew it."

"Yet, you told him what everyone thought?" I asked.

"I told him what they thought, and I told him what *I* thought." She sipped her wine, then added, "The man had trouble with boundaries. I suggested there are plenty of other churches, ones with more liberal views."

A black crackle landed on the arm of an empty chair behind us. A sadness overcame me and didn't go away when the bird flew off. I asked Mary Ellen where she was the night

160

Rooster was found. Rummaging in her purse, she pulled out two concert tickets. "I took my son Eddie. He loved it."

Gator and I parted with Mary Ellen shortly after.

"So," Gator said, "don't sound like he was no pedophile after all."

"Maybe not."

"Only maybe?"

"No proof either way makes it a maybe. We have other parents and boys to question. I've already made appointments with Dave Kelly and Larry Cooper for tomorrow—still trying to get T-Strap's mom. Let's see what we think after that. By the way, Tobin Peterson and I are having supper at eight."

Gator swore under his breath and rolled down his window.

29

When I got back to the inn, I leaned a long time over the dock railing, staring into the water below thinking about child abuse, drugs, and death. As my thoughts whirled and eddied, my emotions took a nosedive. I remember gazing into the Boston Harbor month's after I'd learned that Will, my boyfriend, had died. A long shadow had darted across the water. A breeze blew across my cheek. It was as if Will reached up and touched me, giving me comfort and support. With my fingers on the spot, I straightened my shoulders, turned and went inside.

I showered and dressed slowly in a dress I'd bought for $3.00 at a local thrift store. I decided to wear my hair down, something I rarely did.

Knock. Knock.

I gave myself a last look in the mirror and walked barefoot across the room. Tobin held a candy box. He wore a white button-down shirt with rolled up sleeves, black trousers, and leather sandals. No sparks flew. Not even one.

I thanked him, told Gar to behave and left the box near his foot.

"How's the investigation going?" Tobin asked, attempting to take my arm as we walked down the dock.

I took a step to the right. "Moving along," I said. "Got any ideas on who shot at us at Stoner's?"

"Not really. Doubt we will. Not much to go on. You?"

I shook my head and almost told him that I suspected Stoner was the shooter. But without proof, I knew he'd think it was another unfounded speculation, so I kept it to myself.

"I hear Gator is shadowing you."

"I hired him to be my second pair of eyes and ears," I said.

"Strange choice. What were his qualifications?"

"Good at fishing?"

He chuckled and opened the restaurant door. "Glad you have someone with you, but I thought you worked with Zen."

I explained that Zen was preoccupied. He said he thought two women working together was far more preferable to a man and a woman. He suggested I put more pressure on Zen to take Gator's place.

"Why, Tobin, I'd almost think you were jealous." I kept my frown to myself.

He quickly looked away as a woman in a long, flowered dress arrived and took us to a window seat. The view was the pass, a couple of abandoned pilings that had been painted like totem poles and mangrove.

We ordered drinks, then Tobin bent forward, smiled into my eyes and took my hands in his. "We're made for each other, don't you think?"

Startled is not a strong enough word for how his intensity made me feel. He apparently felt my shock because he freed my hands and made light of his comment.

"Whoops. Gave myself away. I'm crazy about you, girl," he sang softly. Ending with, "Dah, dah, dah. Daah."

"Listen, Tobin. I don't feel that way toward you. Okay?"

His smile did not dissolve. It just dimmed. "I understand your feelings. Don't worry. I won't push you. You don't want me to think you're loose. I get that."

163

The skin at the base of my hairline itched. I reached up and scratched it. "It's not that at all. I don't want you to get the wrong idea," I insisted. I rubbed harder.

Tobin gazed into my eyes, nodded and sipped from his wine glass. All through dinner he was his usual knowledgeable, charming self. I don't think he noticed that I had very little more to say.

Later, at the inn, he did a silly dance step and left.

Inside, I leaned against the door struggling against a thought I didn't want to solidify.

Don't think that. Don't!

30

The next day, when Gator and I arrived, Dave Kelly was under a car. All we saw were his lower legs and shoes. When he heard me say his name, he glided out from under the Prius.

His handshake was solid like his small compact body. His hair was redder than mine. I couldn't help but see Rooster laid out on the slab.

"Ah, a fellow Irish country mate," he said. "What county?" he asked.

"Cork," I answered.

"My mom was from Cork. Hah, small world. But, my dad, he was pure Afric American. Thus the Baptist church. No, catechism for me," he said. "My dad wore the pants in our family." He winked and glanced at Gator.

"Gator's the name. Pure reptile. Both sides."

He laughed and grasped Gator's hand with enthusiasm, then asked us to follow him into the office. "Danny will be here in a sec. Have a seat. He said he'd talk to you."

We sat in two chairs against the wall near a file cabinet. Two shotguns filled a gun rack hanging over the cabinet. Dave sat on the edge of his cluttered desk. "I got ta get that car done within the half hour, so let's skip the small talk. What'da ya want to know?"

"What you thought of Jonah Henning."

"Sleazebag." I noted that the tone of his voice had hardened.

"Did you think him capable of hurting a kid?"

"That guy knew how to play by their rules. The kids loved him, but he was rotten to the core all right."

"How so?"

"I moved down here from Mississippi back in the early seventies. My folks hated that state. Too many racists. They figured they'd get killed if they stayed." He picked up a cloth from his desk, wiped a spot off his hand then tossed the towel into a wastebasket near the door.

"One night Danny comes home talking about how Rooster was from Mississippi. How he'd been some ace Nam hero. How his school buddy, Stoner Taylor had come to their group meeting and told his life story. A bell goes off in my head. I usta keep a scrapbook. I pulls it out and thumbed through it and bingo. There he is. Different hair style, different name, but same guy. No doubt about it."

Fascinated by the turn of events, I waited for him to continue.

"The newspaper went crazy over the story of the civil rights workers who'd been killed the summer of '64. Eighteen Klansmen were suspected of being involved. Their pictures were plastered on page two of one issue. Taylor was the third one from the left. No doubt about it. It was him. Only seven were arrested. Steve Taylor, as he was called then, wasn't one of them. They said he disappeared without a trace, you know, like those people who like to fake a suicide so they can start a new life somewhere else. Well, he was a close buddy of Rooster. That's all I needed to know. The guy had to go. I wanted him nowhere near my kid."

"Do you still have that scrapbook?" I asked.

"You kiddin`? Think I'd toss it?"

"Can we see it," I asked.

He grinned. "Thought you might ask that. Got it right here." He stood and walked around the desk, unlocked and pulled open a drawer. He withdrew a large black scrapbook, opened it to the proper page and handed it over.

I don't know how Gator was feeling, but my heartbeat marched way too fast. Sure enough. There was Stoner.

"Do you have a copy machine?"

Dave pointed with his head toward the file cabinet. I stood and went that way. The dusty piece of equipment was hidden behind it. "Did you tell Rooster what you knew?" I asked, lifting the lid and placing the scrapbook just so.

"Nah. Just went to that meeting and voted "yes." If he hadn't left, you can bet your flip flops that he woulda wished he had. I was fixin` to broadcast the news all over the county, even the state."

"Where were you the night Rooster was shot?"

"Out fishing."

"With who?"

"No one. Just myself and a six pack of beer."

The outside door opened. Dave lowered his voice. "He doesn't know anything about this," he said. "Go easy. He worshiped the guy. He's grieving real bad." He took the book and slid it into the drawer. I folded my copy and put it in my pocket as Danny strolled into the room.

Dave introduced us, excused himself and returned to his work. Danny sat on the same edge of the desk as his dad had.

"Dad said you're investigating Rooster's murder."

"That's right."

"The guy was like rock solid. Anything I can do, count me in."

"I assume you knew there was a move at the church to get rid of him?"

He grimaced. "Adults. They're such fools. Can't take any competition. They woulda got over it."

"That musta made you pretty mad at your dad, him being on the side of getting rid of him," Gator said, watching the boy closely.

Danny shrugged. "My dad's cool. I'm sure he had his reasons. But he woulda come around. Rooster was a cock. He wouldn't of folded."

"So you don't think he would have hurt a kid?"

"Ole Roost? No way. He had our backs."

"And you don't think he was planning to leave the church after he was asked to leave?"

"No way."

"Did you know about him helping the Kirkpatrick boy?"

"You mean helping with the online courses?" He shrugged again. "Hell, bravo to Roost. The kid is a football star. Anyone who could help him play college ball should get a medal."

"His folks didn't look at it that way."

"See what I mean? Adults are square and uncool."

When I asked him where he was the night Rooster was killed, he said he'd been working on a car. No, no one else was around.

Thinking our own thoughts, Gator and I finished our interview.

"So, we're trying to discover if any of these church folks have motive, means, and opportunity, right?" Gator asked as we left the garage.

"Yep."

"Motive, I understand. Opportunity—you got to see if they have an airtight alibi. But, what exactly does "means" mean?" Gator asked.

"The ability of a person to commit the crime."

"Like, having the money to hire an assassin? Or owning a shotgun and being able to pull the trigger?"

"I wondered if you'd noticed them," I said.

"Hard to miss."

"That's quite a motive he gave us."

"Yeah, if I was black and I knew a former Klansman was in my church teaching my kids, I might want to kill him myself."

"I just had a terrible thought."

"What's that?"

"What if all the church members are lying? What if Dave told them what he learned and they got together and did something about it? Knowing they'd be questioned, they each made up a plausible story."

"Why, girl! Now you're thinking. I had that very thought, but didn't expect you to think it."

I stopped in my tracks. "Hey! Why not?"

"Ah, come on. You lean heavily on the "people are basically good" side. Do you really think a group of Bible thumpers would get together and decide to commit murder?"

"Well . . ."

"That's what I thought. Doesn't mean they didn't do it though."

"No it doesn't." But oh how I hoped they hadn't. I thought back to the day I'd talked to the pastor—how he hadn't told me about the pedophile accusation—how if it hadn't been for T-Strap I wouldn't have known about it. Could the pastor be in on the execution? I couldn't help but shudder.

Gator lit a cigarette and sighed heavily. "At least, love," he said, "you're becoming more realistic. You got to stop feeling sorry for every person who hands you a sob story in a bait bucket."

I'd gotten similar advice before, especially from Hawk. Occasionally from Grandma. Often from Will. My mom, on the other hand, didn't think I showed her any empathy. Lately, I'd even felt some sympathy for her. Oh, well. Did this mean I was growing up? Becoming more adult? Didn't know if I liked it, but life has a way of not leaving you behind.

Personally, I'd prefer to be back playing with my crayons or jumping rope in the sand at Grandma's house.

31

A half hour later Gator and I followed a white egret down a path that lead toward a marina where we were about to question two other church members, Larry and Jed Cooper. Gator reminded me to be broad-minded. I assured him I realized I had a bad trait for a PI and would work at overcoming it. He shook his head and flipped his cigarette into a bush.

"Hey!" I said. "That's not nice!"

"There you go again," he growled. "You don't got "tough" in you."

"Surely you know I'm a karate black belt!"

"Yeah, and I'm Muhammad Ali. Bet those flip flops really hurt your opponent."

I didn't have time to argue with him, so I merely glared and walked away—taking what I hoped was a Gloria Steinem type of stride.

The marina buzzed with incoming and outgoing boat traffic. A group of raucous tourists climbed out of a ferry.

As we neared the boat, a man with dreadlocks, whom I assumed was Larry Cooper, sat in a director's chair. He raised a bottle of beer.

Gator gave him a friendly nod. We introduced ourselves and he told us to call him Coop. Reaching in the cooler beside him, he pulled out two beers and handed them over. Neither of us refused.

"Much obliged," Gator said, snapping off the lid.

"Whata day, huh, mon?" Coop said, waving his bottle at the blue, cloudless sky.

"Wonder what the boaters are doing in Canada right now?" Gator added.

They clicked their bottles and drank. Apparently, I wasn't to be part of their male bonding ritual. I stepped to the right and looked out over the water. It was way too perfect a day to be investigating a murder. I should be standing in front of my easel recreating that view.

Minutes later, Coop and Gator walked my way.

"So you're here about Henning's death?"

"Yeah, we've been hired to investigate his murder."

"How can I help?"

"We understand you went to a church meeting concerning ole Rooster," Gator said.

"Oh, yeah. For sure. Voted to have him kicked out of the congregation, along with almost everyone else at that meeting."

"And why was that?" Gator asked before I could.

Coop's eyebrows raised. "Would you want a mon who could be a pedophile teaching your kids?"

"Seems like 'could be' ain't exactly evidence," Gator said.

Coop looked toward the door to the boat's cabin. "I know. Don't think I wasn't aware of that. It wasn't like we were calling the cops or anything. We just didn't want to take the chance it was true. We didn't want him around our kids anymore."

"I see," I said. "Do you have any idea who started this rumor?"

"Nah. And, as I said, we weren't sure it was a rumor."

"So, this guy, who is a devoted caregiver for his handicapped ex-wife and his two kids, who has volunteered his free time to spend with your kids, is ousted just because someone starts a *rumor* that he might be a pedophile?"

Coop, seeming more than uncomfortable, did not reply.

"Where were you the night Rooster was killed?" I asked.

"Out fishing."

"Anyone with you? Anyone see you out there?"

"Nope."

I set down my almost-filled bottle of beer. "Can we speak to your son?"

"Hey, Jed come out here and talk to this woman," Coop yelled.

We walked over to the boat. A teen dressed in baggy black hopped off. He had a snake tattoo on his neck and a ring in his nose. It was hard for me to imagine this Goth attending church or a summer camp. His painted black fingernails were the same hue as his hair and eyebrows. So very *not* Florida, I thought.

Gator climbed onboard.

"My name's Jessie," I said.

"So?"

"Hey, be cool," his dad warned.

Jed's nose ring sparkled when the sunlight hit it. Gator stuck his head in the cabin door as I followed Jed down the dock. Coop leaned against the boat, facing us.

I saw no reason for small talk with a teenager who obviously didn't want to talk to me, so I jumped right in. "I understand you knew Jonah or Rooster Henning."

"Yeah, so?"

"I assume you know he was murdered?"

"What'da you want?"

173

"I'm creating a profile, trying to figure out who might have wanted him dead."

"Yeah, so?"

Great. A sparkly conversationalist. Obviously not a chip off the ole` block.

"Can you tell me about him?"

"Skag."

I frowned and stepped closer. "Skag? I'm sorry I don't know that word."

"Inhabitant of the Planet Pandora. Eats everything in their reach, then spits them out. Lots of heads, mon."

"I take it these inhabitants are from a game?"

He looked at me as if I was half dead, more than half dead. "Borderlands," he mumbled, most likely already dismissing me.

"The guy wouldn't buy that Jesus was black. Fool." He opened his mouth wide in a yawn, showing me a gold tongue ring.

I swore he did it to see my reaction. I kept my expression neutral.

"Adults are hypocrites," he said.

"You think Jesus was black?"

He expelled a sound that told me what he thought of me—about one on a scale of ten.

"Did you think Rooster had, well, special interest in boys?"

He pulled a rolled cigarette from his over-sized pants pocket. I started to ask if he were old enough to smoke, but refrained myself.

"The guy wasn't cool, but he was no boy freak."

"What did you think when you heard there was a movement to get rid of him at the church?"

174

"Like shocked, mon," he said in a girlish voice.

"So it didn't surprise you?"

"Nothing adults do surprises me. Never met one I could trust."

"Not even Rooster?"

"Especially not Rooster. The man was way too good to be true. You ever meet his ex-wife? That guy was takin' care of a crip, man. You can't trust nobody who would take care of a crip."

Isn't taking care of someone with a disability a Christian thing to do? Was this some strange generation gap? I had the feeling that the kid liked to say things for shock value. I decided to not respond to his last statement.

"Your dad?"

He frowned. "What about him?"

"Do you trust him?"

He tapped his cigarette against his pant leg. Apparently a text message came in. Jed withdrew his phone from a clip on his pants, read it, wrote something and headed for the boat.

"It's just a stage," Coop said, circling his bottle toward the cabin where his son had just disappeared. His breast pocket drooped from the weight of a cell phone, something I hadn't noticed before.

"We all went through one," Gator said, inhaling deeply on his cigarette.

I told them that Jed was the first teen who hadn't thought Rooster was cool.

"Jed never takes the popular stand. He may not have been Rooster's biggest advocate, but he never missed anything that he led at church." He picked up a sponge.

"I wouldn't have guessed that."

175

"The kid works hard at his tough image," Coop said. "He thinks I'm too soft, so he has to be different. Truth is, he's softer than me. Got it from his mom, rest her soul."

"What did you think of Rooster?" I asked.

"He dug his own grave."

"Did you get the impression anyone at the church would want him dead?"

He turned his back to me. "Nah. We're all God-fearing Christians."

Sure they are.

"So were most Klan members," I said, shooting Gator a look.

Coop looked at me sharply. "Strange subject to bring up."

"Why?"

"No reason. Just strange."

"You ever hear of Rooster being connected to the Klan?"

"What? The Klan? No way!"

"Didn't say he was. Just a rumor I heard."

He lowered his head.

Like Dave and Danny, neither Jed nor Coop had alibis that could be checked. They each said they'd spent the time alone.

Gator and I left soon after.

"So, what did you think?" I asked.

"You hit a nerve with that Klan comment. Caught him by surprise. Well done."

"I thought so too and he lied like a throw rug."

"Yep, and there's another thing."

"What?"

"There was a shotgun in that cabin."

32

I was quiet as we drove back to Matlacha. With the Klan connection now proven by the newspaper article and photo that Larry showed us, I was sure this was the foundation for Stoner having nightmares and perhaps Rooster's reason as well. But was Stoner the killer? Had Rooster found Jesus and needed to confess his past sins, thus exposing Stoner? Thus compelling Stoner to kill him? Or had another person connected to the civil right murders exacted revenge? Or was it one of the church parents or teens who swallowed what looked to be a lie that Rooster was a pedophile? My bet was on Stoner. His hiring of me and the shooting at his house could be just a way to steer the cops and me away from thoughts that he was involved. But, as usual, I cautioned myself not to jump to a conclusion too fast.

"What you mullin' over?" Gator asked.

"Speculating on possibilities, no answers yet," I said.

"I'm thinking it was Turnstone."

My eyebrows arched. "Why?"

"That guy has a short fuse. If he thought his son even came anywhere near a pedophile, he'd strike out like a rattler."

Gator had a point, but still . . . I shared my theory that Stoner may have killed Rooster to keep him quiet about their involvement in the Klan and to avoid imprisonment.

"Guess we plain don't know yet, huh?" Gator said.

"Guess not."

"Wonder if the fish are bitin'? You need me tonight?"

"Nah."

177

"Good thing."

This fishing thing amazed me. How could Gator run off to fish in the midst of a murder investigation? Then it struck me. Didn't I escape to my room to paint or sketch or both? Didn't I power walk every day? Perhaps fishing time was Gator's best thinking time. Like my art time and my walks were mine. Stepping away from an investigation to think was an important step in the analytical process. Hawk had taught me that. It seemed Gator had a few things to teach me as well.

After a quick hamburger at Bert's, I went back to my room to do my accounting. I was hardly into my work when someone tapped on the door. Without setting down my pen, I peeked through my blinds and saw it was Stoner Taylor. I glanced at the clock on the nightstand: 9 p.m. Leaving the chain intact, I opened the door a crack. "I'll have your statement in the morning," I said.

"I need to talk to you." His eyes caught mine, then lowered toward the dock planks.

Behind him, a man and a woman were fishing. Their presence assured me that stepping outside wouldn't put me at risk of being killed by this potential killer.

"Give me a sec," I said, shutting the door. "Keep your eyes on him. Okay?" I said to Gar before unlatching the door and stepping outside, leaving it ajar.

Stoner was smoking. The fisherman and woman were baiting their hooks with shrimp bigger than my thumb.

"I'm in the middle of something," I said. "Make it fast."

Truth was, even with the fisher folk close, I was still a bit on edge. Stoner really could be a murderer and I sure did like living.

"There's something I need to tell you . . ." He hesitated as he gazed out over the water.

I leaned back against the railing. "So, tell me."

"It's about me and Roost. Well, maybe more about me. Something that might help you find his killer."

"Okay, so shoot."

And no, I didn't mean that literally.

"Back in Mississippi, me and Roost were dumb kids. We did dumb things. We followed our folks. It wasn't right."

"You mean during the civil unrest?"

"Yep. We had just graduated when those college kids came down that summer. Me and Roost beat up more than our share of blacks. We joined the Klan. We were even suspected of taking part in the deaths of those Freedom Riders, but we didn't have nothin` to do with that."

"Nothing?"

"Not a damn thing. But before leaving Mississippi, we'd both been threatened. We've lived watching our backs ever since."

"So, you think someone from Mississippi recognized him and wanted him dead?"

I, of course, already knew that someone had recognized Stoner and put two and two together.

"Yep. That's what I'm thinkin`."

"And that person who shot at us the other night, might be after you too for the same reason?"

"Yep." He tossed his cigarette into the dark water.

I also knew that Rooster had told his fishing buddy Faulkner that he was half black but didn't want Stoner to know.

"Did you know that Rooster was half African-American?"

Stoner looked like I'd hit him. "Nah, can't be."

"He was. No doubt about it."

179

He drew a long drag from his cigarette. "Damn! For real?"
I nodded.

"Jesus! Beating all those black kids and lighting those fires. Damn! How could he do that? Oh, Lord, Lily was right."

"Right about what?"

"She never liked Roost. Said he had a streak of the devil in him. But I wouldn't believe her. I figured if she knew the real me, she wouldn't like me either. I'm sick of living this lie."

He reached into his pocket and pulled out two one-thousand dollar bills. "This should cover a chunk of your bill."

Whirling lights flickered around the bridge, the pass, the inn.

"That would be my ride."

I frowned. "The cops?"

"Yeah, I don't want to rot in hell. I called them before coming here. Roost convinced me to help him sell the pot in the area. I guess it's time to pay the consequences. Besides, with me there, my family will be safer."

Heavy heels pounding boards echoed off the dock planks.

Stoner tossed his cigarette. "You find Roost's killer. He might have had some bad seed in him, but don't we all? Roost was my bud. I left Lily with some cash to pay the rest of your bill when you get the sucker."

33

My eyes popped open. I sat up and yawned. With Stoner no longer a suspect I felt like the road had been swept cleaner. I'd get the killer. I was sure of it. Climbing out of bed, I dressed for my power walk. Clear sky. Bright Florida sun. Life was good. I opened the door. A fly flew out of a bouquet of zinnias sitting near the yellow Adirondack chair and landed on my nose. I stared aghast at the flowers. Ohmigod! No! My stalker! My eyes filled with tears.

Slamming the door shut and locking it, I phoned Gator. He arrived in less than five minutes. Talking a mile a minute about my fear and the delivery of the new gift from my stalker, I let him in. He sat on one chair. I collapsed in the other.

"What do you think we should do?"

I raised my head and gazed at him steadily. "First, get rid of those flowers, will you?"

Gator went outside. I began to pace.

Splash! Sigh. Dang!

"Okay. Now what?" Gator asked, sitting at the table again.

"Maybe we need to switch our energies toward the stalker," I said.

"I got an idea."

"Okay, soldier, what?"

"Has anyone tried to find out who the woman was who escaped from the van?"

I stared at him, speechless. Why hadn't I thought of that?

"The woman in the van?"

"Yeah, but you sure it was a woman? Did you see her face?"

I shook my head, remembering. "No, she kept it covered by the hood of a yellow rain slicker."

"What made you think it was a woman?"

I pursed my lips. "I don't know. Her size. I remember the person being tall. Wore gloves. Masculine boots. Hmm. Why did I think it was a woman?" I asked myself.

I lowered my eyelids and put myself back in that ditch. Rain pouring down. Van overturned. Head popping up from the window. Ah, the bangs. I looked at Gator. "She had red hair and bangs."

Gator ruffled his hair then ran his fingers through it. "Like this?"

Bangs. He now had bangs. Great! He was doing it again—making a fool of my rational thinking abilities. Grrr.

Of course men could have bangs, especially when it was pouring. Hair would be plastered to the head. Dang. Maybe the passenger had been a man, not a woman. I put myself at the scene again. Then . . .

"No! It was the voice. She had a high-pitched, woman's voice."

Gator started to open his mouth.

I put up my hands. "Okay, I get it. You're right. Men can have voices that sound like women, especially if they're excited. Crap!"

It wasn't just the driver of the van or the passenger who had been excited. I had been a nervous wreck myself. Was it possible I had made the wrong assumption? Oh, yeah.

"Maybe we should take a break from the murder investigation and concentrate on finding out who keeps sending you those flowers," Gator said, pulling out another match from his box.

He was right. I took his head in my hands and kissed him on the forehead, then backed up in dismay.

"Hey, when did you have your last shower?"

Eww.

He inserted the match in his ear and turned it.

34

Since zinnias didn't grow in Florida unless someone had a greenhouse, I googled flower shops in a twenty-mile radius. Gator tackled the phone book. Once we had our names, we cross-checked them, making a master list. Our questions: Had anyone ordered a bouquet of zinnias in the past week to be sent to the Bridgewater Inn in Matlacha? Did anyone know of a private grower with a greenhouse who sold zinnias? We divided the list in half.

We discussed the possibility of checking grocery stores. But, again zinnias, for Florida were hard to come by; we doubted grocery stores would carry them.

Of course flowers could be ordered online. But I was putting my money on the fact that my stalker didn't use the internet. A long shot, but we had to start somewhere.

When I left on the Flower Shop Mission as Gator dubbed it, I wore my lucky tan cap and decided to take Gar along for good luck as well.

However, shop after shop, the answer was the same negative response. When I returned to the Bridgewater Inn to say I wasn't in a good mood was putting it very, very mildly.

I unstrapped Gar and tucked him under my arm, grumbling my displeasure. I turned the corner. "Hey!" It was the cobra-like threatening Russ Beadle. I stepped back two steps and gave him the evil eye. Not that he moved. Not at first. Working my lips into a sputter, I yanked Gar to my front and using him as a shield, tried to scoot around Beadle.

"Hey! You!"

Hiss.

"Yeah?"

"It's Gator."

"Gator?"

"He's in the hospital."

"Christ, why didn't you tell me. What happened?"

"Been trying to call."

I frowned and pulled out my phone. The screen was black. Dead battery.

"He was found beat up real bad," Beadle said.

Beadle followed me to the hospital in his truck. Reminding myself that I needed a car phone charger, I asked him to phone Zen. He already had.

Gator was hooked up to several IVs. His head was wrapped in white gauze. His left arm was in a cast.

"He's strongly medicated," the nurse said. "He may stay out for some time. The police just left."

"He'll be okay, right?" I asked.

"He's had internal injuries. I can't say. The doctor will be in later."

I went to the bed and picked up Gator's uninjured hand. "Hey, it's me," I said in a soft voice. "What's crackin`?"

But Gator's eyes didn't flutter. His fingers remained immobile. Beadle pulled up a chair for me and I sat. He stepped back toward the window and folded his arms over his chest. We stayed that way for quite some time. Footsteps told us someone was coming. Sheriff White and Tobin Peterson walked into the room. Tobin was holding a black leather bag.

I stood.

The sheriff looked at the unconscious Gator, at Beadle and then at me. "Let's go into the hall," she said. She nodded toward Beadle. "I'll speak to you later." We went to a corner

185

of the hallway. Zen rushed through the double doors and headed straight for me. We hugged, spoke briefly about Gator, and she hurried into his room.

The sheriff eyed me up and down. Tobin held a pen and pad of paper. He gave me a concerned look before the sheriff began speaking.

"I understand Gator was working with you on the Henning case," the sheriff said.

"That's right."

"Do you know what he was up to today?"

"I had more zinnias delivered. We were trying to find out who had delivered them. We were going to various flower shops in the vicinity."

"Why was this delivery from your stalker not reported to us? Don't you want our help?"

I shrugged.

The sheriff folded her arms over her chest and scowled.

Tobin turned his body slightly to the left. I could no longer see his face. The sheriff continued to give me the evil eye. "If you want our help with this, you have to keep us informed. I don't need to remind you of that."

"Yeah, sure," I mumbled.

"Do you have any other news to tell me?"

"Remember the woman . . . er, person at the accident? Gator and I think . . ."

"Gator and you think?"

"Yes, sheriff. We think that that person, whether man or woman, might be my stalker."

"Man or woman? If my memory is correct the person was reported to be a woman."

"Yes, I know. But I never saw her face." I turned to Tobin. "Did you?"

He thought for a moment, then said, "Actually, no. I guess I took your word for it that it was a woman."

The sheriff looked disgusted.

"Well, anyway . . . if it was a man, he could have been my stalker."

Could have been. I realized how thin that statement was. In fact, this was just a wild guess. Wild guesses have very little credibility in the world of those searching for a criminal. I was sure the sheriff thought the same thing. I didn't even have an intuitive hunch on my side, I was just fishing from a sinking boat.

"For now, I'm concerned with finding out who attacked Gator." The sheriff gave me a solemn look then nodded at Tobin. He pulled a plastic bag out of the satchel he'd sat on the terrazzo floor and handed it to me.

"That was found on Gator's chest."

A zinnia.

"It appears your stalker is not of the harmless variety. Looks like he may have become jealous of your male partner in crime."

Before I returned to the room and sent out Beadle to talk to them, the sheriff assured me that I would now have police protection and she advised me to stay out of the investigation.

When Beadle came back into the room, Tobin stuck his head inside and asked if he could see me in the hallway. The sheriff was gone. Tobin put his hands on my shoulders and tried to pull me to him, but I shook him off. I didn't need coddling. What kind of woman did he think I was anyway? A silly wimp? "I'll be okay," I told him.

He stepped back. "You need me, I'm here," he said in an official tone, then turned and walked down the hall. As he went through the door, another officer came toward me. My body guard, I was sure. I returned to the room. The officer remained near the open door.

A nurse bustled in. "He needs to sleep." Her glance swept over us. Come back tomorrow. He'll most likely be awake by then."

Zen and I protested, but the nurse insisted. Beadle stepped forward. "You two get out of here. I'm staying," he said.

The nurse drew herself up to her full five-foot-two height. "It would be best . . ."

"I'm stayin`," Beadle growled from his towering position.

We left Beadle sitting in the chair, arms folded over his chest, no longer looking like the snake I usually associated him with, now a gruff, protecting grizzly bear.

35

"Gator's going to be okay," Zen said.

"I know he will." I knew we were doing our personal method of prayer to ask for this to be true.

We were at Zen's sitting cross-legged on a newly painted bench near her fire pot.

"Fill me in," Zen insisted.

I told her about the flower delivery, our decision to question flower shop workers, and the zinnia found on Gator's chest.

Zen continually pulled at a strand of her hair, a sign something was wrong, and not just with Gator. "I should have been with you."

"You were busy. Don't worry about it."

She snatched a glance at Gar, dropping her hand to her lap. Her expression was more than sad. Her eyes glistened with emotion. Maybe I knew Zen too well. "It's over?" I asked softly.

She nodded.

"I'm sorry."

"No, you're not, but that's okay. I'm here for you now." Her face puckered. "Poor Gator."

I sensed there was some "poor Zen" in those words as well. "The cops will get him."

"Sure they will."

We looked long and hard at each other before we parted for the night. Me, to sleep. Zen to do whatever Zen did.

36

Zen's single-wide trailer was set at the end of a cul-de-sac. A canal with a cement seawall covered in barnacles served as a backyard. Other trailers lined both sides of the road. I opened Zen's front door and asked for strength for the next leg of my journey. The smell of burnt dead leaves was strong. Stepping inside I threw a glance over my shoulder, double checking that my gun-toting shadow was in place. He was. I hoped he'd have no reason to come inside. The smell was a dead give-away. I didn't want Zen hauled into jail. She was on the phone apparently talking to someone at the hospital. "Gator's sleepin`," she said, pocketing the phone and taking a long drag. "But should be awake soon."

"Okay, let's go to the hospital first," I said.

Zen nodded.

As I drove, I noticed Zen seemed nervous, not sad as Gator's situation would warrant, but antsy—almost anxious. Was she afraid of being attacked too?

"Our tail is right behind us," I said.

"I see that." She snatched a look at me. "I hear you're seeing Tobin Peterson," she said so softly that I asked her to repeat herself.

"Tobin? Not really."

"He's an odd one," Zen mumbled.

"How so?"

"He's one of those too-smart people."

"Meaning?"

"He never graduated from high school, but ended up in grad school at Stanford, then went to a police academy and became a cop."

"Like, he's some kind of genius?"

"Could be."

"How do you know this?" I rolled down my window.

"We usta date."

I looked at her sharply. "Excuse me?"

Zen shrugged. "Not long. He wasn't my type."

I'm not sure what I thought about having slept with a reject of Zen's.

I glanced in the rearview mirror. The copper was only a car length behind. "How come I didn't know?"

"You're only here six months out of the year. Lots can happen in six months."

I drove a couple miles without talking, then: "You want to talk about it?"

"Not much to say. We didn't click. In fact, I always got the feeling that he dated me to learn more about you."

"But I met him just before I left last year."

"Seemed to me that you were more on his mind than me."

The information didn't set quite right.

"You ever date Gator?" I asked as I parked the car in the hospital parking lot.

"Not hardly. We're second cousins."

I hesitated before withdrawing the car keys. "Didn't know that either," I said.

"There's a lot you don't know about us," Zen said, slamming her car door.

By "us" I assumed Zen meant the year-round residents of Matlacha and Pine Island. She was right. Being somewhere only six months out of the year draws lines, creates boundaries and walls, even some resentment.

By the time we'd stepped off the elevator on Gator's floor, I had convinced myself that I would be a more authentic friend. One that asked questions about the personal lives of those they wished to welcome into their life. I also decided to pay closer attention to Tobin Peterson and how he acted around me.

Gator was sitting up in the hospital bed with a tray of food set in front of him. Russ Beadle was scooping red jello out of a plastic container.

"You eatin' his food?" I asked.

"He's not hungry," Beadle said, standing. "I ain't had jello in years."

I shimmied over to the corner and pulled over a second chair. Beadle took his spot by the window.

Zen sat on Gator's left side. "'Bout time you stopped sleepin' on the job." She reached into her over-sized shirt pocket. "Brought you a present." She pulled out two chocolate brownies wrapped in cellophane and handed them over. "They're special." Wink.

Gator laughed, but I could tell the reaction hurt. He held up his cast. "I don't need this thing."

"Nurse said it was broken."

"Hell, I set my own arm back in '97 down in the glades. Remember that, Zen?

"Yeah, but you weren't beat up everywhere else then."

Beadle reached over Zen's head and snatched up Gator's covered plate of food. "Anyone want this? It's scrambled eggs and bacon."

We shook our heads. Beadle swept up the paper-napkin wrapped silverware and retreated to the window.

Gator continued to talk. "Me and Zen here had a business back then collecting baby gators."

"Hah! More a hobby than a business. We were lucky to make enough for a burger and beer."

"She made us quit. Said those gators belonged in the wild. She was right. I know for a fact that gators don't belong all trussed up in no building."

I leaned forward. "Any chance you saw who attacked you?"

"Nope. He came at me from behind. I was out before I knew what hit me."

"You know it was a man?" Oh yeah, I felt vindicated asking this question.

Gator took a while to answer. "Nah, don't even know that. Could have been some he-man woman. I seen plenty of women strong enough to tackle the likes of me."

I had too. I was one. Thanks to my karate skills. So there.

"If I ain't released by those docs by mornin' I'll be leavin' anyways. I got my rights."

Beadle swiped the back of his hairy hand over his crumb-dotted lips. A piece of toast hung from his mustache. "Hey, man, you got internal injuries. You're staying until they say you can leave," he said.

Gator lifted his free fist and shook it at him.

"Besides," Beadle said, "I don't mind this free food one damn bit."

This was one time I was glad that Russ Beadle was built like a garbage truck. It was obvious he had appointed himself to hog-tie Gator to the bed until he was damn well enough to leave. I was more than relieved.

37

Later, before getting in the car, Zen tossed me a "wait a sec" look and walked away. When she returned I smelled the distinct odor of burnt dry leaves. I tipped my cap toward my nose. "You shouldn't smoke in public."

She shrugged. "Whatever. Even Tobin smokes."

"Tobin Peterson? No way. He's a cop."

She smirk-smiled. "You're such an innocent."

Zen and I went to every flower shop still not checked off on our list. None had an order for a bouquet to be delivered to the Bridgewater. None knew of a private grower. So the stalker had ordered online. Dang. Foiled again.

Zen insisted that I tell her everything Gator and I had done in the investigation before Stoner was arrested. I told her about the pedophile accusation given by the church parents, what we had found out about the Klan connection with Rooster and Stoner, about Rooster being half African-American, about his Caucasian, blind sister in Fort Myers who wrote him checks to help out his wife, about how Jack Lesan had given him big bucks too, about his sister's husband who disliked Rooster whom I had yet to interview, about how we had speculated that the church members were told about the Klan connection and that they may have signed a pact to have one of them murder him. I ended by saying that my first suspect had been Stoner as I thought he might have offed Rooster who he feared would go public with their past crimes—how that line of thought had been proven wrong and why. Then I decided we should return to my room where I

194

could get to my notes. I opened my iPad and began by outlining my new suspect list and notes:

The mystery person who'd been riding in the van. Motive: Keep Rooster from getting her/him arrested. For what? Being part of the marijuana scam.

The church parents: Motive: Rage from fear he had molested their kid or they were enraged with his past Klan activity and decided to seek revenge. Gator thinks the killer could have been Turnstone.

An unidentified person from Neshoba County who sought revenge.

Sadie's boyfriend. Perhaps had been confronted by Rooster. Could have lied about not being jealous. Or could have been angry about Rooster not using his money as intended.

Rooster's brother-in-law who was tired of him bothering his wife for a handout. (Very weak motive).

Without giving Zen, who was sitting cross-legged on my comforter, time to talk, I continued.

"As far as the mystery person in the van, we nor the cops have had any luck tracing who it is. No fingerprints, including Rooster's were found in the van. Apparently they wore gloves. Strange, considering they were in the South. Before this, we interviewed all of the parents. At first, as I said, Gator thought one of the dads was volatile enough to act in a fit of rage, but he and his wife were off on a vacation when Rooster was killed and Hawk confirmed this, so no-go there. Of course, a hit man could have been hired, but in this case, that's hard to imagine. As far as the church members doing it? I admit, I hate to think it's possible, but Gator was quick to remind me I'm a sucker."

I waited for Zen's protest. Got known. Thanks, I'll remember that. "So, that's an option. The idea of an unidentified person from Neshoba County seeking revenge is still a viable possibility too."

Zen's eyes roamed the room. "So what needs to be done?"

"I still need to talk to Rooster's sister's husband who had a grudge against him and to T-Strap's mom."

"T-Strap?"

"Yeah, he's a kid from the church. Apparently he, like most of the other kids, thought Rooster was a saint—at least that was his story. For a while there, I thought Rooster might be selling pot to his boy-only youth group. From everything I've gathered about Rooster, I'd say that was a strong possibility."

"Disgusting," Zen said. Then: "What about your stalker? Are you scared? Had to be him who creamed Gator."

Sure I was scared. Sure I wanted him arrested. But how would that ever happen? A light bulb began flickering in my head. I stood. "You know what I'm thinking?"

"What?"

"I think I'll go to the sheriff and fill her in on the details of my or our investigation."

"Why?"

"Maybe something I've found out can help nail the killer. It's not like I have to be the one who corners them. Why shouldn't the law be the heroes?"

Zen unfolded her legs. "With you being the prey of a sociopath, you're probably right on the money. You've got enough danger surrounding ya," she said. "Let's go."

I held up my hand. "I think I'll do this on my own. Don't worry, I've got my shadow. I'll catch back up with you later. Keep your cell on. And don't forget to get it charged."

What I was hoping was that the next time I saw Zen, I'd be shadow-free.

On the way to the police station I got a call from Gator. He was at Bert's. Grinning, I took my toy horn out of my side pocket and began to play a hopped up version of Yankee Doodle Dandy.

38

Everywhere I went, John, my cop shadow went. It was like having a tick attached to my forearm. I could only hope I didn't get Lyme disease.

When I pulled in front of the station, John parked beside me. "Take ten," I called out amicably, pulling the XXX-sized sweatshirt I had tied around my waist tighter. He grinned at me like a kid just handed a piece of fudge. I wondered what he would be doing if I didn't have a mad stalker, possibly killer, on my tail. Probably watching reruns of *CSI* in his squad car.

John did not follow me inside. "The sheriff available?" The dispatcher made a call and told me to go right in.

The sheriff motioned for me to sit. "I trust Officer Richards has your back?"

"If we were any closer we'd be arrested for indecent exposure."

Tapping a stack of papers on her desk, she gave me a thin smile. "What can I do for you? I hope you haven't had another stalker incident."

"No. None." I crossed my legs. "I thought it was time to share my investigative findings with you."

She leaned forward and picked up a pen. "Excellent. Shoot."

When I finished, she leaned back in her chair.

"Interesting. Most of your findings concur with ours. We, too, are feeling the past Klan connection is an important link. But that's all I am free to say at this point. I'm sure you understand. Thanks for coming in. Rest assured I feel positive we will get the killer."

That's when I told her my decision to stop my investigation, citing the fear I felt because of my stalker's aggression as the reason. She said she was glad I'd come to my senses. "By the way," she added, "how's your friend?"

I had to smile. "He left the hospital this morning."

"I'm surprised they released him."

"They didn't."

She grinned. "My dad was like that. Thought he knew better than anyone else."

I studied the portrait of the sheriff on the wall over her head, deciding it had been taken at least ten years prior. I looked at her badge, at a photo where she was standing beside Tobin Peterson and two other deputies. Zen's conversation about Tobin came back to me. My intuition pulsated. I gnawed my lip, glanced at the photo again, and hesitated another second or two. Wow, was it possible? Yeah, it was. But I cautioned myself to not name any names. Not yet. Not without proof. I returned my attention to the sheriff who was looking just a tad bit impatient.

"There's one more thing. Looks like the only way we'll catch my stalker is through me, right?"

I could see I had her attention. Her fingers intertwined and she rested them on the documents.

"So, if we can lose my shadow, John, the odds of him showing himself increases by a high percentage, right?"

The sheriff rubbed her cheek. "You'd be willing to put yourself at risk like that?"

I gnawed on my lip. "I've been at risk since it started. Why is now any different?"

"Have you forgotten what happened to Gator?"

199

I drew in a deep breath. Of course not. But I'm Margaret Murphy's granddaughter and her best pupil. When you start something, she taught me, you stick with it to the bitter end. If you don't, you'll go to your grave with regret and you'll never pass on to the other side and experience any peace. Your ghost will roam the earth trying to make amends, like— forever. And that's something I just don't want. No way. Besides, as long as I'm stalked, when would I have the right mindset to paint? Like, never.

Raising my head, I shot the sheriff a look. "I'll trust that you'll be lurking in the background."

As I said the last word, a cloud drifted over the sun, causing the room to darken.

Great. Just great.

39

I left Sheriff White's office sporting a bulletproof vest, but my cop shadow remained at the station. Losing my girlish figure wasn't that appealing, but the sheriff wouldn't agree to dismiss my bodyguard any other way. Since I had arrived with a very, very large sweatshirt I slipped it over my head. The sheriff advised me to wear one until the vest was no longer necessary. She would also have undercover cops on my tail.

I pulled open the car door and got in behind the wheel, then frowned. A folded piece of paper lay on the passenger seat. I picked it up, drawing in my breath. A poorly drawn yellow zinnia filled the white space. Dang it! I left the car and walking my quick walker steps, reentered the station. Not stopping at the dispatcher's desk, I rushed along the corridor and burst into the sheriff's office.

"What the . . . ?"

In four long strides, I stood in front of her desk and handed over the picture. "This was in my car. It had to be put there while I was talking to you."

The sheriff stood, dropping the paper on her desk. "Stay here. Don't go near the window."

Like that was something I would do.

The next hour was spent asking questions, searching every building, every bush, every car or truck for a suspect. None was found. I wasn't surprised. My stalker was more than clever. That was obvious. Most likely, the sheriff said, he had pulled up, delivered his message, and then quietly driven away. No one had seen such an occurrence, but that had to be the answer. Intuition told me it wasn't.

When the sheriff finally returned to her office, I could tell she was shaken. "I'm assigning John to you again."

"No, you are *not!*" I insisted. "This is exactly what we want. To flush him out. He's getting more brazen. He'll make a mistake soon."

"I can't disagree there."

"I have no reason to believe the stalker wants to hurt me."

The sheriff went to the window. "You're most likely right. Stalkers don't usually want to hurt their victims. They want to possess them. But when they find out that person doesn't share the same feelings, they can become violent and the violence is often directed at the one they love. Also, remember what happened to Gator."

"Oh, I do. I most definitely do. But that was probably an act of jealousy."

The sheriff turned and faced me. "My point exactly."

It was time—time to say what I'd been thinking. "Is Tobin Peterson around today?" I asked.

She looked away then considered me again. "You think . . . ?"

I raised my hands. "Probably not, but, well . . . Is he?"

"He's off-duty today, but came in about an hour or so ago. Said he had some paperwork to catch up on." The sheriff's face paled. "You really don't think . . . ?"

"I don't know what to think."

"But you've been dating him?"

"I'm not sure that dating is the right word."

The sheriff returned to her desk. "Okay, but . . ."

"I may be wrong."

"Officer Peterson has been an exemplary police officer."

"I'm sure of it, but how is it he's always the first on the scene? At the van accident? When Rooster was found dead? When Zen, Stoner, and I were shot at? When that note appeared on my car seat?"

Sheriff White drummed her desktop as she considered. "Well, there was a complaint that was dismissed from a woman a couple of years back . . . He may have some issues where women are concerned." She stopped drumming. "So, well . . . I'll agree to having him watched, but not by one of our deputies—that would raise too much undue suspicion." She bit her lip. "There's this guy I know . . ."

I leaned forward and interrupted her. "How about Zen?"

"Zen?"

"Yeah. She's actually perfect. He knows her. Knows we are friends. She could just show up wherever he is and I don't think he'd be suspicious."

"She couldn't just show up where there was police business."

"No, I suppose not."

The sheriff pushed back into her leather chair. "Here's what I'll do. I'll assign myself to be Peterson's new partner— tell him I need some street time. That will cover his days. I'll let Zen take care of his after-hours." Her brows remained furrowed. "But I repeat: I'm doing this to suppress your concern. As I said, except for that one complaint, Tobin Peterson has always been an exemplary police officer."

I nodded, wondering how many other women had said "no" to Tobin without him accepting the answer.

"As far as the plan," I said, "Gator is out of the hospital. I know he'll help Zen. With those two on his tail, Peterson will think he's become the most popular cop in town. And when they have to be invisible, I'm sure Zen and Gator will be up to the task." Well, that was a stretch, but . . . whatever!

"It's important he not suspect we're watching him. Unless we catch him in the act, we have no proof. Without proof, we can do nothing."

"But if you're always with him, how will he be able to make a move?"

"Don't worry. It's a well-known fact that Peterson has little faith in my abilities as a sheriff. It won't be hard to convince him I'm incompetent. I'll give him plenty of opportunities to be on his own. At least he'll think he's alone."

40

It was time to bait a trap. If the fox was a cop that was caught, so be it.

Oddly enough, I'd had an early lesson in trap baiting. When I was eleven Grandma Murphy had taken me to a woods that she and her sister had often frequented as teens. I don't know why she thought it was important for me to know how to catch a live animal, but she obviously did.

Grandma's advice was simple: When trapping an animal, find out what the critter liked best and make sure the trap was big enough.

"So, how are we going to trap him?"" Zen asked as we climbed into Gator's truck. He was more than raring to get back into the "Get the Stalker" saddle.

"We'll search his home. Stalkers take pictures, keep souvenirs."

"We'll break and enter?" Zen asked, looking dubious. "A cop's place? What if he comes home and finds us?"

"That won't happen. I'll distract him. Invite him out. Tell him I've reconsidered my decision to break off our relationship. You two will get into his apartment and see what you find."

"This is the same guy you suspect beat me to a pulp?" Gator asked.

I nodded.

"And you plan to go out with him like he's some kind of guy you're interested in?"

"Why not?"

"Got a better idea?"

"Maybe Zen could stay with me," I said slowly.

"He sees me, he'll suggest another time," she said.

I sighed. "You're probably right."

We gazed out the smudged windshield, thinking.

"How about this," Gator said, "You knock on his door, catch him unaware and tell him you need to talk. Before you get into the car, Zen shows up."

"And I bodyguard her?"

I could tell this idea appealed to Zen.

"That might work," I said, "Once he's out the door, surely he wouldn't change his mind when Zen arrives."

No one mentioned what each of us knew: That would put Zen in danger too.

"Just give me an hour," Gator said. "Pickin` locks is a piece of lemon meringue cake."

I took out my cell phone and within minutes with use of the Internet, had Tobin's address.

"Okay, he lives on Hancock Parkway. If we're in luck, he'll be there. You go on ahead. I'll follow you. Here's the address." I handed him a torn piece of paper. "Be sure and park as far as possible from the apartment building."

Tobin answered the door on my second knock. His face lit up. "Why, Jessie. What a surprise. I didn't know you knew where I lived." He glanced over his shoulder, stepped outside and shut the door, closing it behind him. "My place is a mess or I'd have you in. I'm amazed you're here."

I gave him a sad smile. "I've been thinking about us." I used my warmest womanish voice. "Can we talk?"

"Why, of course. Come on."

We neared my car. No Zen. No bodyguard. And of course I hadn't worn my bulletproof vest. What was I thinking?

"Why don't we go in the cruiser," Tobin said.

I agreed, all the time looking over my shoulder.

But, no Zen. Definitely no Zen. And no undercover. I mean, how undercover did the sheriff mean? Spying at us out of a garbage can?

I let Tobin do all the talking as he drove as I struggled over concern for Zen. What if the real killer had grabbed her? I glanced behind me. No following vehicle. Great. Just great.

I didn't pull away from Tobin's hand when he took my elbow as we walked into the restaurant. Two tables were occupied. Surely Zen was safe, I assured myself. My job was to keep Tobin occupied for an hour to give Gator time to search his place. I pushed Zen out of my mind and talked. I was amazed at how my mouth could run off when it felt the need to. I hardly let Tobin say a word. At one point he reached for my hands on the table and again I didn't pull away. I glanced at the clock. "Thanks, Tobin. You don't know how much this has meant to me. I'm sure I'll sleep better tonight."

"I'm just glad I was home. I'm here for you. Remember that. I'll call you tomorrow." He didn't touch me. He sent no bad obsessive stalker vibes. But I knew quite well, sociopaths are capable of fooling almost anyone.

Zen didn't answer her cell nor return a text message. Gator had no cell phone. I drove back to Matlacha watching for Gator's truck, praying when I saw it, that Zen would be sitting beside him.

The parking spaces in front of the inn were filled, so I pulled into Bert's Pine Bay Gallery. Gator and Zen were most likely at Bert's. I'd go there, then move my car later when some of the tourists had gone home.

As I walked through the door, Gator and Zen waved to me from the bar. The relief I felt made me grab the edge of the pool table. She's not hurt. Wasn't attacked by Tobin. Okay. Okay. I meandered toward them. "I don't see a cast on your legs," I growled. "Some bodyguard."

"Dang it, Jessie. I got thinkin`. Seems like Peterson wouldn't like me joinin` you, might blow off the whole thing and return inside, so I climbed into the back of your car and tossed your paint tarp over me so's I'd be close. How was I to know you wouldn't drive?"

I rolled my eyes. "Who paid you to think?"

Zen sniffed and chugged her beer.

Gator was not doing a very good job of suppressing a grin.

"What did you find out?" I asked Gator.

"He likes Aretha Franklin and Salted Nut Rolls." He swiveled toward me. "Did you know those are hard to find?"

"The music? Or the candy bars?"

"Candy bars, of course."

"No photos. No souvenirs?"

Gator scratched his whiskers. "Nope. Got to admit, I like that candy too. Had to snitch a couple. Next time you see him, would you ask where he's getting them? He's got several boxes."

Disgusted, I turned abruptly on the seat and stood, heading for the door.

"And one more thing."

I hesitated. "Yeah."

"The bedroom door has a hole in it the size of a fist. The fridge is badly smashed in several places. My guess is, this guy has an explosive temper, one he finds hard to control."

I nodded and hurried away.

"Least we know one more important thing," Gator called out.

I hesitated. A pool ball dropped into a pocket with a loud thud.

"It probably ain't him."

Without turning, I gave them a wave.

If it wasn't Tobin—who was IT? Was there any connection between my stalker and the killer?

"Please make it not so," I whispered.

41

The inn's dock was quiet . . . tranquil . . . just as I liked it. Meditative music drifted across the water. I was sketching. Trying to tell myself that I didn't feel any tension in my shoulders. But I knew I was fooling myself. Inside, I was anything but serene. Being stalked by an unknown person had me constantly feeling like I teetered on the ledge of an underwater crater. Not being able to nail Rooster's killer didn't help either. I was glad I had ended my investigation. At least when I drew I could seek out refuge in my imagination. I sighed and paused my pencil. Smudged out a line. Continued. Stopped again. Eventually, I was sure I would paint again.

The drawing was that of a faceless human in a hoody. I shaded in the outstretched left arm. Each finger was adorned with a ring.

I set down my pencil, closed my sketchpad and stood. A boat horn sounded. A disagreeable odor coming from beneath me made me crinkle my nose. I glanced over the railing and saw the half-eaten carcass of a large shark bobbing in the waves. Startled, I took two steps back and froze when a hand grasped my shoulder.

"Start walking."

A sharp object pricked my lower back. The grip tightened.

"Say even one word, make a face or a movement that causes anyone to stop us and I'll push this knife home. Understand?" The tone was harsh, guttural. I couldn't tell if it was a man or a woman's voice.

Another snarl. "Don't look back."

I took a mini-step toward the front of the inn. One quick move and I could disarm the intruder.

"Stay close."

I gulped, tripped over a dock board and grabbed the railing.

The attacker swore. I straightened. My fists clenched, preparing.

"Go ahead, try something. Think I don't know you're a karate expert?"

Resigned, I let my arms drop loosely to my side. "Where are you taking me?"

"See that black van? Head over there."

Without moving my head, I glanced right to left. Surely someone would see my dilemma? Surely someone would stop to talk to me. But the street and parking area were empty. An osprey squawked. A pelican flew low. I stepped over a gopher tortoise.

The knife blade pricked my skin through my thin T-shirt. I winced. "Don't even think of turning around." My arms were wrenched behind me. Tape was wrapped around my wrists. Frisking me, my cell phone was removed from my shorts' pocket, then the door slid open. "Get in, baby girl."

Baby girl? Words of endearment? So, this was my stalker. But who was it? The voice was that of someone who was or had been a heavy smoker. So not Tobin, or else he was disguising his voice. I still couldn't tell if this was a man or a woman.

The side, back and window between me and the driver and passenger seats were covered in black film. The filthy carpet was cluttered with McDonald's paper cups and hamburger wrappers. The driver door opened and closed. The engine started and the van backed up.

I banged on the blackened window between me and the driver. "Where are you taking me?" I yelled.

"Shush it."

Unable to use my hands, I pulled back my legs and kicked at the door. We were still going slowly enough for me to hop out, if only I could get the door open. Thud. Thud! Thud!! The vehicle rocked. "Ouch!" My ankles exploded with pain.

The van slowed and pulled to the side of the road. Cars passed. I continued to kick. The window dividing the front from the back slid open. The barrel of a gun appeared. My eyes widened. I dropped my feet to the floor, crunching a clear plastic cup.

"You know what the words "shush it" mean? I don't plan to hurt you as long as you cooperate. But I'll do whatever is necessary to keep you with me. We belong together, you and me. It's a destiny thing. Our courtin` days are over."

Courting days? All the fear the stalker had caused, had been a form of courting? Good Grief!

Tears welled up in my eyes.

42

"Who are you?"

"I'm your soulmate. Some might even say your doppelganger." Low ruthless laughter came from the cab.

My evil twin? I have no evil twin. I don't even *believe* in evil twins. Surely you can't be kidnapped by a being you didn't believe in. That's science fiction stuff. What would Hawk, Luke, Jay, Zen, and Gator think when I told them this news. I didn't even want to think about the sheriff's reaction or Grandma Murphy's. Having a plaster of Paris gargoyle as a companion was one thing, but having a stalker who obviously had surrendered rational capacity? How embarrassing.

The barrel of the gun waved up and down. I put my hand on my chest. "That's crazy," I said with a bitter, biting tone. Why couldn't I be a love object for someone more reasonable? Wouldn't you know, Grandma? Geez! Mom will just love this.

The divider slammed shut.

Pushing down my urge to kick again, I settled back in the seat as the van's tires crunched off the gravel and entered the flow of traffic. I would have a better chance of escape when we got to where we were going. I was sure of it. I concentrated on the van's actions, hoping I would be able to retrace this journey. That is, once I overpowered the utterly pathetic stalker who seemed to be way too overly prepared with weapons.

We were heading toward the Cape. Not far away, the van took a right and the road became bumpier. Within minutes, the van stopped, the engine turned off, and the driver got out. The door slid open a couple of inches. "Turn around facing away from me."

I caught a glimpse of a familiar oval galvanized tub and a rusty boat trailer. Had to be Smithy's neighbor. I swiveled around and was immediately blindfolded. Something was fitted over my shoulders. My tan cap was taken off and some other type hat was pushed down tight over my forehead.

"Get out." The words came out as a hiss.

As soon as my feet hit the ground, I was pushed roughly forward. "Hurry up." I tripped but caught myself. "Okay, stop right there."

Metal scraped metal, then rank stink of mildew and mold assaulted me. Pushed. Yanked. Until another door opened and the force of a shove landed me on a mattress. "Hey, take off the blindfold," I yelled. "This isn't fair."

A door shut.

"One hen," came a chilling whisper.

My blood thickened into cold pudding. I struggled to sit up. Whatever the stalker had wrapped around my shoulders dropped off. I fought against the tape around my wrists.

"Remember, Jessie? Remember?"

I pursed my lips, frowning.

"Two ducks."

My heart pounded.

"Three squawking geese."

I tugged harder at my restraints.

"Four limerick oysters."

A classmate! Someone who knew about that more than embarrassing day in school. It couldn't be Tobin.

Seething with anger and fear, I jumped from the bed and rushed toward the door.

"You sick creep!! Who are you?"

"I'll be back, Jessie. Don't worry. I won't leave you for long. We're meant to be together. Bye bye, baby girl."

"Don't call me baby girl!"

Footsteps retreated. The distant sound of a door opened and then shut.

I was alone.

I put my forehead against the door and recited, "Six pairs of Don Alfredo's tweezers. Seven brass monkeys from the secret crypts of Egypt." Mortified, I slid to the floor. "Eight hundred Macedonian warriors in full battle array."

I had been eight and in third grade when the teacher directed me to the front of the class to recite the announcer's test that Jerry Lewis had long ago made famous on the radio. The fear of being in front of so many faces was more than I could bare. I peed my pants before dropping to my knees sobbing. Laughter cut through my heart leaving razor blade thin cuts. Mom said I deserved what I got. Grandma let me stay home the next day. But from that day on, I was teased mercilessly. You would think that I would be over the shame, of the feeling of being less than the others in the class, but I was not. Probably would never be.

Why, if this evil monster loved me, would it taunt me with it?

Why?

43

I sniffled and closed my eyes, attempting to stretch and twist the tape. The muscles of my upper arms bulged. I stopped and counted to ten, visualizing the third-grade class. Starting with the front row of seats, one-by-one I remembered names—faces. Had a classmate acted odd toward me as we grew older? Had anyone been overly attached? I could think of no one. I grunted and twisted. Sweat beads popped out on my head. I had had nothing to do with my classmates since high school graduation. I hadn't liked any of them since the teasing began. I twisted harder. None of them did I ever think was a friend and certainly not a soulmate. Evil? Squeezing my eyes shut, I cringed with my effort. Oh yeah, every . . . one of them . . . I thought were . . . ev . . . il.

There! Got it!

With a final yank, I was free. I rubbed my wrists.

I got up from the floor while pulling off my blindfold. With it came a floppy straw hat that I assumed my unidentified stalker thought would hide my blindfold from gawking neighbors. A cockroach scurried across the floor, disappearing under the mattress.

If this stalker really loved me, why would I be tossed into such a dirty hole? Which one of my classmates was that twisted? Because obviously one of them was. The only one who came to mind was Tommy Davis. He often pushed me too hard on the swing at recess until I squealed. Once he had stolen my lunch. But Tommy was shorter than me when we graduated. Unless he'd done a lot of growing after then, it couldn't be him. This person was close to my same height.

Tossing the hat on the bed beside the dirty shawl that had been over my shoulders, I took a look around.

The room was empty except for a bare mattress on top of a metal frame. The terrazzo floors had lost their shine ages ago. The closet door was open. Several haphazard, dilapidated boxes filled with musty smelling clothes spilled out into the room. Rifling through them, I discovered nothing I could use as a weapon. I returned the boxes to their former state and went to the window to look through the cheap broken blinds. Metal hurricane shutters canceled all chance of a view of the outside. Anole and cockroach droppings and congealed dust coated the blinds. I grimaced and wiped my hands on my shirt. The door was locked. That I had already expected.

Although I was still a prisoner, I felt confident. I had surprise on my side. I went back to the mattress, saw how stained and filthy it was, and instead sat on a pile of newspapers in the corner with my back against the wall.

44

I don't know how long I sat like that, but it was long enough for me to doze off. Luckily my eyes popped open at the sound of a door shuddering. Pushing up from the floor, I retied the blindfold over my eyes, pulled on the straw hat, positioned my hands behind me, and sat on the bed—ready for stalker bear.

The doorknob moved slightly, but the door did not open. Footsteps retreated. Pots and pans rattled. Water ran. I remained seated.

Continued movement in what had to be the kitchen gave me courage to stand and tiptoe toward the door. Raising my blindfold, I stooped and peered through the keyhole. I could see the back of someone with red hair wearing jeans and a large T-shirt.

Come on, turn around. Show yourself.

The kidnapper walked out of view. I straightened and returned to the bed. At least I knew what body type I was facing—one similar to mine. I wondered if the person knew karate. If we would be an even match.

Footsteps neared again. The doorknob turned. I steeled myself for action.

"Brought you some soup." But the tone changed from pleasant to angry in a split of a hair. "Why, you wily thing."

Knowing I was had, I jettisoned off the bed, threw off my blindfold and charged. The room was pitch black. Crack!! "Uh!" I dropped to my knees. Shaking my head, I wobbled back and forth, attempting to stand. Another loud crack sent me sprawling flat on the floor. My eyes closed.

When I awakened I was in the middle of the kitchen tied to a wooden ladder-back chair by thin wire. I moved my wrist and the wire cut into my flesh. I groaned. The room looked distant, coated in a thin layer of film.

"I wouldn't do that if I were you. Wire ain't as forgiving as tape." Turning, my stalker faced me.

I gasped as I stared at my face, my hair, my body.

The woman smiled. "Hard to believe, ain't it? Docs can perform miracles today. Absolute miracles." She walked toward me with a bowl and spoon in hand. "Hungry? And for your information, you can scream and scream if you feel like it. This neighborhood is deserted. All the snowbirds have left. I mow their yards and watch their houses. This one usta be my aunt's but she hasn't been back since the last hurricane. Can't blame her, I admit. The damage was extensive."

Where was my undercover? Where was Zen? Gator? Where was Tobin?

45

Hours passed—then what had to be a full day. I was taken out of the chair only twice. Three times she forced me to take a pill. I became more and more lethargic physically, but my mind was sound and active.

The second day she helped me take a sponge bath. She was gentle, soothing, but firm. I was to stay in the chair until we left. It was a shame, she said, she had planned to let me sleep in the bed, but I had proven myself to be untrustworthy. Apparently she had stocked the house because she never left nor ventured outside. She often hummed as she played solitaire. Occasionally waved at me as she passed. Seldom spoke.

The third night I watched her pacing back and forth in her bedroom. The walls were covered with photos of me. Her voice became louder with each turn of her body. It was as if she were rehearsing. Weirdly enough, it seemed she was talking to me, but she wasn't. I watched and listened as tears patterned my face. When she made a derogatory comment about my cap, I'd had it.

"Hey! I love my cap! And I'm never going to totally give up painting! Get that in your head right now!" I yelled.

But she was in some kind of weird sociopath zone. She ignored me, her droning voice continuing. I caught the word "zinnia." I wanted to scream again. This woman was bonkers. I would never pick a zinnia again, as in NEVER!

Tears streamed down my face. "Couldn't you please just shut that door," I said softly. "Please, just shut the door."

The mattress squeaked and her muffled dialogue droned on.

"Please," I begged. "Please. Please. Stop talking to yourself! Dear God, please. Oh, please."

Opening the nightstand drawer, she withdrew a bottle and a hypodermic syringe from a box. Glancing my way, she smiled and held up the needle. "This usta be my dad's." She pushed up her right sleeve. "Want a hit?"

I shuddered, closed my eyes and prayed.

46

The next morning I awoke terrified I'd been shot up with heroin. But except for the fact I felt weak, I didn't feel drugged. I assumed I'd fainted at her offer. I sure didn't remember anything after those words. I wasn't even sure what it would feel like the morning after having been injected. All I knew is that I seemed okay—well, sort of, kind of—under the circumstances.

When she came into the room, she began telling me a story as she poured cereal into a bowl. The story was one I'd never paint.

She had loved me for as long as she could remember. As I had figured out, we *had* been classmates since the third grade. Her name was Teresa Bellon. Didn't I remember her? We had been lab partners in science class in fifth grade. The Teresa Bellon I knew had been a quiet, shy girl with thick lensed glasses who came to school in too-big clothes. She hardly ever spoke and hung her head most of the time.

She'd been, she said, living with her mom since high school graduation while saving the money to get the operation that transformed her into my twin. Once she had recouped, using Craigslist, she secured a ride with a man named Rooster who was driving from Colorado to Florida. She hadn't known, she said, that he was hauling pot until she'd gotten in the van. Being so close to me in the ditch had disoriented her. Although she was on a mission—to find me again so we could start our life together, the suddenness of being so close made her react as she had done. She rolled up her sleeve. "Course I have this problem too. The cops wouldn't have taken it lightly I figured, so I scooted." As I knew already, her arms were riddled with needle marks.

Creepy. Double creepy. It was like watching myself crazy talk, but knowing it wasn't me.

Sometimes when I dozed I imagined Jay Mann, my former sculptor boyfriend, in a long white flowing robe holding me. Once I saw myself kayaking toward an island. Another time Will was encouraging me to continue my painting. But when I was conscious, for sanity's sake, I concentrated on the murder case.

I looked at her. She was playing solitaire. Was she a killer? Or just a crazed sociopath madly and obsessively in love?

"Did you ever go into the bait shop in Matlacha?" I asked.

"Sure. The guy in there was real friendly. Thought I was you. That's how I found out where you were staying. He told me to watch out for the manatees at the inn. That they could often be seen from the dock."

"He was a friend of Rooster's, the guy you hitched a ride with."

"Yeah, I thought that was an odd coincidence. Saw the pics with him and the owner's kids on the wall behind his head. Seemed like a pretty okay guy. Anyone taking on a chicken's name is okay with me." She took another card off the deck.

"He was murdered," I said.

"Saw that in the paper. A shame." Her calm, casual demeanor and words told me she hadn't killed him. I was relieved. At least she was no murderer. That was something. Just crazy as all get out.

223

With her looking so much like me I wondered how she traveled around Matlacha without getting called out on her appearance. Surely someone had seen us at almost the same time and been curious.

"Anyone ever seem confused in Matlacha when they saw you? You being now my twin and all."

She raised an eyebrow and gave me a look that said I was dense. "A wig and wiping off the freckles, baby girl. That's all it took to disguise me. You don't remember, but I was number one in our class. I wasn't born yesterday."

47

Later that day Teresa was wiping my mouth after feeding me when someone knocked on the door. Calmly she put down the paper napkin. Going to a cabinet, she pulled out a brunette wig and put it on, smoothing out the bangs. Then she went to a small mirror on the wall, and rubbed off her freckles. She winked at me. "Be right back." She started away, but apparently changing her mind, went to the drawer near the sink and pulled out a roll of electrical tape. Tearing off a piece, she secured it over my mouth. "Not a peep. Hear me?"

I nodded, pleading with my eyes for her to free me. She smiled and patted my check. "God, baby girl, I love you so."

She walked through the door, pulling it closed behind her. She'd left my cell phone on the table. I waited a couple of seconds and then began rocking the chair back and forth to turn myself around. One more half-turn and I was there. Leaning dangerously forward, I switched on the phone, clicked on my last message to Zen, tapped the forward icon and typed quickly. *Help near Smithy's place black van in driveway.* I hit "send." Smithy was a friend of both Zen and Gator. They knew where he lived.

I swiveled on one leg, then rocked again. I almost returned to my former position when the kitchen door popped open. Almost.

"Be right with you," Teresa yelled. She glanced at me, then the phone. Eyes ablaze, she stomped over and slapped my face. "Don't even think of trying that again." Placing her hands on the back of the chair, she tilted me to the side and lowered me to the floor. "Stay that way until I get back. One move and you'll regret it." She left again, closing the door with a loud thud.

Whew! Luckily, it seemed, she hadn't realized what I had done.

Okay. Okay. Find me. I'm waiting.

I could hear talking, but couldn't make out any words but the tone of the visitor. GATOR! It was GATOR!

The door swung open and Teresa reentered chuckling. "That was the feller I ran off the road and pounded into raw hamburger 'cause he was smooching up to you. Had a mind to conk him over the head again for good measure, but restrained myself. He won't be back. Don't matter anyway. We're leaving tomorrow crack of dawn. You want a drink?" she asked as she pulled me and the chair to an upright position. "I'm hittin' the sack early."

After she took me to the john, she settled me back on the chair in the center of the kitchen floor and went into the bedroom. I could see her Glock on the nightstand near her head. I sunk my chin onto my chest and closed my eyes, waiting.

Click. I raised my chin. Click. I turned my head. The doorknob moved. I licked my dry lips. Click. Inch by inch the door opened. My gaze darted to the bedroom where Teresa slept.

A current of fresh air hit me as Gator's gnarly face appeared. I gasped. He placed his finger to his lips. I nodded toward the bedroom. He put up his pointer finger, signaling he understood and opened the door wide enough for him to enter. Slowly, ever so slowly, he tiptoed toward me. My eyes darted again to the open door. Zen's face emerged. Her eyes blazed with fire when she saw me and my predicament. I prayed she wouldn't call out and awaken Teresa. Gingerly she crept forward.

Gator motioned for her to take one side of the chair. He took the other. When he gave a nod, they lifted me and half tiptoed and half sidestepped toward the door they had come in. They didn't stop until they had me in the back of Gator's truck parked two doors down. Zen hopped in beside me and Gator slid behind the wheel. He put the truck into reverse and we rolled down the driveway. At the end, he started the engine and burned rubber while Zen pulled the tape from my mouth.

I felt whoozy, relieved and angry all at the same time. "What took you so long?" I asked over the roar of the muffler.

"Tarpon are in. We went fishin`," Zen yelled back. "Hey, you look like a damsel out of distress strapped to that kitchen chair. Can't wait til *The Eagle* gets wind of this. Reckon we'll make the front page." She pulled out her new cell phone. "Smile." She touched the screen. "Love this phone, they say it's smarter than me."

I gave her a look fit to kill. She winked. Moving behind me, she began to untwist the wires. I advised her to wait. My body was weakened from sitting so long and by the pills Teresa had given me. Hard to tell how it would react once it was free. And we were in the back of a speeding pickup no less. I really didn't want to be lying on the floor beside the fishing poles, stinky bait buckets and slimy lines and crab traps wrapped in seaweed.

But I wasn't so drugged that I couldn't laugh at my current situation and raise my head to the stars and say "Thank you." Wasn't so weak that I couldn't hug Gator and Zen once they had taken off my restraints at the hospital where a doc looked me over and told me to go home and get some rest. Wasn't so wasted that I didn't want to join the sheriff on the speedy ride to arrest Teresa.

"She might be gone by now," the sheriff said as she took a curve on two wheels.

I grabbed the armrest. "Maybe, but I don't think so. When that woman goes to bed she takes two sleeping pills and snores like a trucker."

The sheriff and Tobin Peterson grinned. Zen chuckled. Gator tossed an unlit cigarette out the window.

"You going to turn on the siren?" Gator asked. "Always wanted to be in a cop car blaring down the highway."

"Don't want to alert her, do we?" the sheriff said.

"Gator said that chick looked just like you," Zen said.

I cringed. "She does. Had plastic surgery. Liked the idea of being my evil twin."

"She on drugs?"

"Oh, yeah. Big time. Heroin. She was, by the way, the woman with Rooster on the highway."

"You're kiddin`," Tobin said.

"Nope. Quite a coincidence, huh? But I'm pretty sure she didn't kill him."

"Why's that?"

"Ah, the way she talked about him. She seemed to like him."

The sheriff and Tobin gave each other a look. Gator quickly turned toward the window.

"Ah, come on, Jessie," he said, "that's enough to think she didn't do it? REALLY!"

I blushed. So shoot me.

After a quick turn to the right, Sheriff White slowed the car and we crept forward. Four houses down, we spotted the black van. The sheriff pulled off the road and turned to look at us. "Okay, you three stay in the car. Peterson and I will go in. Once we have her under arrest, you can join us, but not before. Got that?"

Without looking at each other, we nodded. They opened their doors, stepped out and took their guns out of their holsters. White went to the front door while Peterson headed around the house to the back.

"Okay, let's go," I said. "Be quiet about it."

Gator, Zen, and I got out of the squad car and hunkering down, ran toward the house as the sheriff made her presence known, waited a minute, then kicked in the door.

Bang!

The sheriff went down on one knee. I was two feet away. Zen three. Gator near the corner of the house.

Creeping up to the sheriff, I grabbed the back of her collar, pulling her away from the door.

Bang! Bang!

Loud thud. Groan. "She got Peterson," Gator mouthed. I motioned for Gator to go to him and wait. Slowly, I eased the gun from Sheriff White's hand.

Her eyes closed.

Zen was now at my side. "Put pressure on the wound," I mouthed, eyeing the door. "Losing too much blood."

For several minutes there was no sound, no sense that anyone was moving. Without speaking out loud, I cautioned Zen to remain silent and still. Teresa couldn't stay in there forever. I assumed she was calculating if there were other officers around. I was hoping she hadn't seen me pull the sheriff away, that she had been too busy with Tobin Peterson. If that were the case and I waited her out, then I had the advantage. Fingers crossed that Gator was a patient man.

229

Would she come out the back door or the front? Time would tell.

I inched up the house wall next to the door, both hands on the revolver.

Crunch. Crunch. Someone advanced. I pursed my lips. Be patient, I told myself.

Crunch.

Wide-eyed and paler than I'd ever seen her, Zen squeaked like a trapped mouse.

I swiveled and came face to face with my twin. The action startled us both. Recovering first, I raised my right leg and kneed her in the gut. She doubled over and I heard the trigger of her gun tick. I slammed my arms and the gun across her neck, dropping her to the floor. Her Glock scooted toward Zen. Zen snatched up the gun and aimed it at her prone body. "Move one inch and you're dead meat," she snarled.

Teresa looked up.

"Eww," Zen said, "this is too weird. It's like pointing a gun at you."

"Hold that gun steady. She's one mean babe," I said.

I knelt in front of the sheriff who groaned and then opened her eyes. Gator walked around the building with Tobin who was holding his shooting arm.

"Hey, didn't I tell you three to wait in the car?" Sheriff White said, struggling to a sitting position.

48

I bit back my frown when I saw Tobin came down the dock with his arm in a sling. He dropped into the yellow Adirondack chair beside me.

"Well?" I said, tapping my sketchpad on my knee.

He dropped a piece of lead into my palm. "A gift from my arm."

I examined the bullet. "I guess she'll be put away for a long time."

"Yeah. I don't think she'll be bothering you anymore." He turned and studied my face. "Feeling better?"

"You can't imagine. How's the sheriff?"

He grinned. "Back to work. Can't keep that woman down. I got more respect for her, that's for sure. Guess I got lots to learn."

We gazed out over the choppy pass. "Are there any more leads concerning the murders?" I said.

His expression sobered, but his gaze remained on a soaring pelican. "Afraid not. The sheriff was banking on your stalker being the killer. But after talking to you and interrogating the woman, White is pretty sure Bellon's no murderer."

I rapped my sketchpad on my knee again where I'd been doodling stick fingers of Rooster, Stoner, his family, and those I had questioned, the sheriff, and Tobin. Each figure had a bubble overhead containing any and all details I could recall. I glanced sideways at Tobin, then bit down on my lower lip and drew a picture of a pie, then twin dolls—the dolls that I'd

231

seen in Stoner's trailer. I dropped the pad into Tobin's lap. "Want a beer?"

He picked up the sketchpad and gave it a good look. "A pie? You hungry for something sweet?"

"Nah, not really. According to Sadi, Rooster loved strawberry pie. For some reason that fact just came back to me."

"Twin dolls? Thinking about your evil twin?"

I gave him a thin smile. "I suppose. And doing that made me remember that there were twin dolls in Stoner's home the night we were shot at."

"Ah, I see. Drawing helps you bring back details."

I nodded. "Sometimes. Want that beer?"

"Sounds good."

I stood. "Study that while I'm gone and tell me if anything out of the ordinary pops out at you."

"I take it something here is causing the skin on the back of your hairline to itch."

I smiled a thin smile. "Something fierce. Be right back."

When I stepped inside the room, my breath suddenly left me and I grabbed the table to steady myself.

Who had motive and means and opportunity? Who was humiliated by Rooster? Who was the first on the scene when Gator, Stoner, and I were shot in the driveway at Stoner's house? Who was known to use pot? Who was really smart and had a perfect cover to sell drugs in the area? Who had an explosive, uncontrollable temper?

"Hey, Jessie, you brewing that beer, or what?"

I closed my eyes for a brief second and then walked to the fridge. I didn't want to think what I was thinking. I didn't want someone I had come to trust and care about to be a murderer. How could I ever trust my instincts again?

Head down, I yanked open the door and pulled out two Guinnesses. Why couldn't people be who you thought they were?

I placed the bottles on the table and snapped off the tops with an opener. Gar sat under the lamplight. I raised a bottle to my lips, stopping in midair as an arm encircled my waist and Tobin leaned toward my left ear. Okay, I told myself, don't pull away. Don't show your fear. He rubbed his nose in my hair. Eww. I slipped out of his embrace gently and stepped away. Alert. On high alert. "No revelation?" I asked in my most controlled voice.

"Nah. I'm not detective material, I'm afraid. No aptitude in the rational thinking area. Just an action man, that's me."

Which, if Zen was right, was a total lie.

I walked outside and he followed. The sketchpad was lying on the blue chair I'd been using. I retrieved it and sat, contemplating what to do next.

Oddly, I felt sadness and strong empathy for Tobin. My mind said I shouldn't, but my heart ignored the advice. It wasn't that I loved him. Our relationship hadn't evolved to that. I could almost hear the bubbles on the page bursting. Pop. Pop. POP!

Grandma Murphy always warned me: Don't trust so quickly. Don't care so deeply. There will be disappointments. Rise above them. Don't let anyone take you down so deep in a well that it takes more than a baker's dozen of days to climb out.

"My, my, haven't we become grave. Penny for your thoughts," Tobin said.

I don't think so, buddy. Not on your life, or mine.

A boat motored by. I didn't look that way, but Tobin did. He almost fell as he jettisoned from the chair. "I can't believe

233

it!! Come on, Jessie. We need to intercept that skiff." And he shot away.

I only hesitated momentarily before following him. As long as all my senses were on alert, I'd be okay, I assured myself. With my karate skills I was at least an even match. Tobin withdrew his gun from under his shirt.

Dang. Why was I following him?

"Where are we going? Who are we chasing?" I yelled as I rounded the inn.

"If my eyes didn't deceive me, this will blow the murder case wide open. I'm sure I know where that skiff is headed. Hurry. No time to talk."

"Tobin!"

"You got your cell phone on you?"

I nodded.

"Call the sheriff and tell her we're heading for the bait shop. Tell her to bring backup."

Hey, what's your theory? I wanted to yell, but he was too far ahead. Dang.

Stopping to make the call, I kept Tobin in my sight. I relayed the message and then the sheriff asked to speak to him. I caught up to him and handed over the phone. Tobin listened, then said: "You won't believe who it …"

Bang! Bang!

In the next second, Tobin dropped to his knees and then keeled over onto his side. The phone slid onto the gravel. I called out and sunk to the ground. Blood oozed from his chest. His gun remained clutched in his hand. "Rooster," he whispered as he closed his eyes.

"Oh, God, no!! Tobin, TOBIN!"

49

"I'm staying," Zen said.

I sat at the table in front of the window in my room in the inn, staring out over the water. "That's not necessary." I'd been sitting in the same position for quite some time thinking about death. If the bullet had entered Tobin's body another inch to the left, he would be dead. The thought was chilling.

"I'm staying anyway." Zen held a paper sack. "I'll crash on that sleeper sofa."

After she got situated she suggested that we go to Bert's, but I just shook my head. I had a vague feeling in my gut that the bar would be almost empty tonight. Word of Tobin being shot in broad daylight had to have everyone on edge. Most likely doors were closed and locked. Why in the world did Tobin think he'd seen Rooster? Rooster was dead.

"Don't worry. He'll be okay."

"I know. The sheriff said he should be conscious by morning and we could see him then."

"Great." Zen sat yoga-like on the bed rummaging through her paper bag. "Want to play rummy?"

"Don't know how."

She held up a deck of cards. "About time you learned. Gator and I usta play every night when we were huntin` in the glades. Come on, get up."

I blinked several times then stood. I felt hollow. Distant. I sat on the bed. My sketchpad lay on a pillow. I ran my fingers over the cover while Zen dealt.

"It's all about getting runs in the same suit and pairs."

I opened the sketchpad and absently leafed through it.

"Earth to Jessie. Earth to Jessie. Is anyone out there?"

I felt my mood shift as an inner door in my mind clicked opened. Pairs. PAIRS! That was it. Twins! Suddenly fully aware of my surroundings, I flipped through the book again and then picking it up, looked at Zen. Zen's eyes were shining. She put down her cards.

"Look at this. Take your time. Tell me what you think." I slipped from the bed and headed for the door, but changed my mind. I really had nothing to say to the deputy outside who was assigned to watch over me, and gazing at the sea or the sky with him standing over my shoulder wasn't very appealing. I pulled on the cord of the window blind and raised it. The constellation Pisces was clearly visible, as was the farther northern constellation, Pegasus. In Greek mythology Pisces was identified as a pair of fish swimming together. There it was again—PAIRS! If things went right, that's what Zen and I would be doing later, working as a team to take down a killer, but with a cop shadow (maybe more than one) in tow. PI me was back! More than back.

Zen read and turned the pages and I began to pace. When Zen closed the book, she looked at me steadily.

"Well?" I said, standing in front of her.

"Oddest thing."

"What?"

"Looking at this, I mighta concluded that Tobin Peterson was the killer."

"Exactly! I did too and was thinking of what to do about it. He was sitting with me on the dock when suddenly he sees a skiff motor by and gets all excited, pulls out his gun, yelling the case will be open wide as he takes off, me following."

"Who did he think it was?"

"The last thing he said before becoming unconscious was 'Rooster.'"

"But that's not possible."

"Yeah. It's not. Or is it? Anyway, obviously I'd come to the wrong conclusion. All the clues had not been uncovered. Tobin was not the murderer. The murderer's still out there. But are there clues on those pages that point to anyone? That's the question."

"Hmm."

"Okay, now that you know this, turn back to this page. Anything stand out to you?"

When Zen raised her head, her eyes were wide. "Why the doodle of the pie and twin dolls?"

"Exactly! I added those doodles just before that skiff motored by. Sadi said Rooster's favorite pie was strawberry, but his poker buddy claimed at one of the last games that Rooster said he was allergic to strawberries. Odd, huh?"

"You're darn tootin! Something ain't right."

"The key word here is 'twins.'"

"Hot damn!" Zen exclaimed.

I pulled out my phone and called Eleanor George. She answered on the first ring. After a very long, pregnant pause, she confirmed my suspicion. The secret had been kept for years. Twin boys had been born—a good twin and an evil twin.

"But how do you keep one a secret?" Zen asked after I hung up.

"Put one in an institution and throw away the key."

"Eww. Wow!"

"Yeah. I'm thinking we need to go to Sadi's. She could be in danger. My guess is that the evil twin wants what the good twin had—a good woman and her kids. You call the sheriff. I got a couple of things in the closet we'll need."

50

Zen arranged her bulletproof vest around her generous body. Then she covered it with a floral decorated shirt in bright greens, yellows, and blues. Turning, she helped me with mine. "These are a good idea. Where'd you get them?"

"Yard sale. They're more than a good idea, there's no telling when bullets will fly."

"Hey!" Zen said, "Do you have to be so graphic?"

"This is a killer with no scruples. Both of us need to keep that in mind."

"Ya packing a gun?" Zen asked.

"Don't have a Florida permit, remember." I slipped on my hat. "You got your gun?"

Zen hung her head. "Had to promise to get rid of it when I was seein` that fool tourist. He insisted on going with me to sell it."

"You kidding me?" I said. "Was it a demand?"

Zen blushed, tilted her head, glanced at Gar and then at me with a question on her face.

I shook my head. "He'll stay here." I'd hidden my blank canvases in my closet where the vests had been. I needed all the Gar mojo he could muster to keep us protected. And there was no doubt his mojo was far-reaching. Besides, Gar didn't own a gun either.

Instinct had told me where the killer would be. And the importance of following my instinct was one rule Grandma Murphy had hammered into me.

51

Every detail was the same: The hibiscus still begged to be pruned. The rusty trike remained near the bottom of the steps. The gravel on the driveway crunched just as loud as I drove over the curb. I could even hear the kids in the backyard.

Zen and I got out, making sure not to slam the doors. I rounded the front of the car. The windows of the trailer were open. Sadi was talking. I touched Zen's arm and we hunkered down in front of the small front porch to listen.

"I…you…I can't believe this," Sadi said.

"Don't try to make sense of it, not now. Just get packed. We'll head for Mexico. We can get lost in Mexico."

A man walked by the window. "Hey, it's …" Zen whispered.

"Shh, come on." Bent over, I headed for a thick grove of areca palms that divided Sadi's yard from her neighbor's, but that were close enough to overhear the conversation.

"But we don't speak Spanish." Sadi's voice was shrill, hysterical.

"Quit gripin`."

Something scraped against the floor. "What should I take?"

"Who the hell cares? We'll buy stuff there. I have plenty of cash. Hurry, woman."

Sadi's answer came out in a whine. "But . . ."

"I hate strawberry pie!" A glass pie pan slammed into the already slit window screen facing the arecas, broke through it and scattered on the ground. The next words came out as a growl. "I said we're leavin'. NOW! Get those rugrats!"

"Who *are* you? You can't be Rooster! He'd never call his kids that!"

Smack. Thud!

Sadi screamed.

"Git off that damn floor and find them or I'll kick the shit out of you!"

A twig snapped. I turned and stared eye to eye with Sadi's girl Ada. In a split second her expression transformed to one of terror and she began to scream...as in SCREAM!

Zen and I took off like cross country runners. We made it around the corner of the neighbor's trailer before the screen door of the mobile home crashed against the outer wall.

"Quit that blasted wailin'!"

The girl now sat in the middle of strawberry pie filling kicking and slapping her hands and the heels of her feet against the ground. "Monster! A red-headed monster!" she bellowed.

I grimaced and growled. "Hey kid, zip it."

Zen chuckled. I gave her a fit-to-kill look.

Our heads turned as Sadi slid past the guy and limped down the steps. She scooped up the girl who never missed a beat as she flailed and screeched. Awkwardly pressing the child to her stomach and chest, Sadi headed for the truck parked at the far side of the house. "Junior, get over here. We're leavin'," she called over the wails of the child.

The man returned inside.

"You go around back," I whispered to Zen. "I'll take the front."

So the guy was bigger than me. And was probably packing. No problem. I had my karate, the element of surprise and . . . forgive me for lying to Zen, Grandma . . . my pistol.

Raising my shirt and withdrawing my gun from my waist holster, I crept up the steps. On the second rung my flip flop came down on a squeaky yellow duck.

Dang!

Before I took another step, the man charged through the door and gave me a powerful shove. I caught myself, but my gun slipped out of my hand and sped across the deck to disappear over the side.

Great. Just great.

I looked up at the shiny blade of a kitchen knife.

NOW, JESSIE! MAKE YOUR MOVE! WHAT ARE YOU WAITING FOR? CHRISTMAS??

Whoosh!

My arm shot out and my fingers gripped the guy around the ankle. He went down like a bag of hammerhead shark guts, hitting his head on the handle of the trike. He groaned and, lucky for me, his eyes closed. But his hold didn't release from the knife.

Releasing his fingers, I tossed the knife near the area where my gun had fallen. Not wanting to risk him suddenly awakening, I pulled his arms behind his back and waited for Zen. Of course I had no handcuffs. No rope. No tape. Nothing to secure those huge burly hands.

Zen came around the corner. She looked at me and with no hesitation, skimmed off her shirt and ran. The two dragon tats seemed to shoot fire from her fleshy arms.

"Here you go. This should do it." She knelt beside me.

Avoiding glancing at the tats that . . . symbolic dignity and power aside . . . always disconcerted me, I wrapped the shirt's sleeves around his wrists and made two sturdy knots.

"Got you, Joshua. Got you!" I whispered in his ear.

A piercing, higher than high-pitched sound more powerful than a speeding hurricane made Zen and I plop down and cover our ears. Zen, of course, locked Joshua's legs in a major leg vice grip.

"Mommy! Mommy! Monsters!! MOMMY!" screeched the little girl over and over while her arms and legs flailed and kicked.

"MOMMY!!"

52

Zen and I sat on the bed in my room munching on a bag of Oreos. Our glasses of milk were half full. The canvas on my easel was filled with the first brushstrokes of a high-ceilinged church interior that housed a sailboat. I couldn't keep myself from glancing at it and smiling. It felt so good to paint again. So good.

"So, why didn't Eleanor tell you that Jonah had a twin when you first talked to her?" Zen asked.

"Joshua was the black sheep of the family. No one likes to talk about black sheep. Besides, the poor thing is in her late eighties and heavily medicated. She probably has some dementia issues. I do remember that when I left I had the feeling she wanted to tell me something else. Her husband came in and the interview ended. I should have contacted her again and should have interviewed him. I planned to, but the case sent me in other directions and I just never got back to covering those bases." I finished off my cookie and swept a pile of crumbs onto the floor.

"Seems like that ex-boss of yours would have uncovered a birth certificate or some such."

"Apparently the courthouse burnt down and most of the documents were destroyed the same day their house was destroyed. Must have been some fire. Hey, there's only one cookie left. You want it?"

"Nah. You go ahead. I'll eat Gar's. He hasn't touched his."

"Go ahead," I said. "He won't mind."

"Jesus," Zen said, grabbing Gar's cookie, "a brother killin` a brother. Sickening."

"Yeah. Real biblical."

"Wonder why he did it?"

"Eleanor said he'd been committed to a mental facility when he was a kid. The family wasn't proud of it. She said before that he was always hurting his brother—once he broke Jonah's arm. Another time he put a classmate in the hospital. Maybe when he was released, he wasn't happy that his bro lived a normal life. Course we'll never know."

"Wow! So weird. You and Rooster both with identical evil twins."

"Yeah, well, I've heard that it's possible we all have a doppelganger somewhere."

"Doublewanter?"

"Doppelganger. Someone who looks so much like us, they could be our twin."

"Even me and Gator?"

I raised my eyebrows and cleared my throat, trying not to chuckle. "Well, let's hope there're exceptions. Oh, and you might want to wipe that milk from your upper lip."

Zen stuck her thumbs in her ears and wiggled her fingers at me. Her white mustache made her look totally child-like.

"My point exactly," I said, smiling. "Sadly enough, the sheriff said that Joshua admitted to being the one who ran his sister off the road and causing her blindness. He didn't even show any remorse about it. He's one evil dude. I don't think any mental institution will ever release him again."

"Glad to hear." Zen swiped at her mustache. "What made you suspect that Jonah had an identical twin?"

"First off, Sadi said Jonah loved strawberry pie, but his poker buddies said he was allergic to strawberries. They also said the last time they'd played poker, Rooster had acted like he'd hardly ever played. When I looked at the timeline, I realized Rooster was in Colorado that last poker night. Someone who could pull themselves off as Rooster had been at that game. Then there was the gift of twin dolls from Rooster to Stoner's kid. What guy gives a child twin dolls without having some connection with twins? The child had no twin, so it stands to reason that Rooster just might have one— one he never talked about, but often thought about. When I phoned his sister she confirmed my speculation. But I told you that part."

"Wow!" Zen said, "Nice deducing!" She dunked the last bit of Oreo in her glass of milk, frowned and said, "Do you think Sadi slept with Joshua thinkin` it was Jonah?"

"I doubt that. Most women would know the difference, wouldn't they?"

Zen giggled. "Maybe they were identical twins in *all* ways."

Jessie shook her head. "I'm not going there."

"What's going to happen to poor Sadi and her kids?"

I sighed. "I heard Rooster's church got together and had a fundraiser for them. Seems they raised enough to help her pay her mortgage and buy food for at least a year. Wouldn't surprise me if they didn't make her cause an annual event."

"Real cool. Oh, I got some fun gossip," Zen said, crinkling up the plastic cookie wrapper.

"Oh, do tell!"

"Guess what Jack Lesan does for a living?"

"What?"

She reached over and turned Gar's face to the wall. "You're going to love this. He's a bimbo for a rich woman who travels the world on her own jet. Apparently she flies in

246

every once in a while and gets her fill of him, leaves a sizeable check on the table and then takes off again. Rumor has it that she's in her late seventies. He's at her beck and call. I guess you might call the poor man a sex slave or manstress or whatever you would call it."

"Oh, NO! How hilarious! He's a boy toy!"

We laughed.

"Don't you love it?" Zen asked, wiping her eyes.

"Oh, God, I do!"

"And Tobin?"

"What about him?"

"You interested?"

"Afraid not. No spark. Besides he doesn't like me paying my share for drinks or meals! That ain't right. And he's way too demonstrative, if you know what I mean!"

"Now," Zen said, "that him paying-the-way stuff I could live with. Oh, God, but the other! Yeah! I 'member when we were datin`. Tobin squeezed my butt on the dance floor. Eww. That, you can bet your tan cap, was our last date." She tossed the wadded up cookie wrapper into the waste basket and stood. "But you got to admit, Tobin's a likeable guy."

I nodded. "He is." I slid off the bedspread and opened the nightstand drawer. "What do you think?" I held up two Mardi Gras masks, one green, one red.

"How fun! Where'd you get `em?"

"Kiwanis, where else?"

"Hey! I want the green one, it matches the color in my tats!"

Facing the mirror, we adjusted them.

Zen grabbed me around my shoulders. "Ain't we something?"

I smiled into the mirror.

"It's okay to be Jessie, sweetie." Grimacing, I glanced behind me, expecting Grandma Murphy to be sitting at the table. *"Go for it, child. Be Jessie. Don't hold back."*

Blinking, turning back to the mirror, I grinned. My eyes began to sparkle. "Hey, let's do something crazy!!"

I was already yanking down my shorts. My fingers touched the lucky stone in my pocket. My grin broadened.

"What are you doin`!?" Zen exclaimed.

I laughed, then removing my mask, stepped out of my shorts and pulled my shirt over my head. Unsnapping my bra, I dropped it on the floor and slipped my mask back on. Giggling, turning my back on Zen, I wiggled my patootie as I dashed to the bathroom and grabbed two towels.

With a "Yeehaw!" Zen tore off her cut-off jeans, her button-down shirt, her bra, her panties and tossed them high into the air. The bra landed on the tan cap on Gar's head.

I tossed her a towel. "We might need these when we get back."

"Back from where?" Zen asked in a hesitant, squeaky, mouse voice.

"Someone left two kayaks tied up to a piling. I'm thinking we should borrow them." Eyes twinkling, towel under my arm, I dashed to the door, threw it open and looked right then left. Coast clear. Great! I tiptoed quick-walk style across the dock and climbed up and over the rail. As I turned to make my descent, Zen stuck her masked face around the corner. "Jessie?" she called in a harsh whisper.

"Get your butt out here, girl!" I whispered back. "And be quiet." I reached my leg out until my toes felt the bottom of the rockin` and rollin` vessel. Tossed my towel behind the seat. "Make sure you put your foot in the center first, and whatever you do, don't knock your paddle overboard."

I adjusted myself on the damp seat. Picked up my paddle. Tipped the right end into the pass. In seconds, I was several feet away from the inn.

Words from Zen shot across the water. "Ohmigod! Ohmigod! Ohmigod! My heinie's cold! Eww!"

After making sure no one was close and there was no danger of being arrested for indecent exposure—at least not this moment—I raised my face to the sky and watched constellations transform into the shape of a woman in a cowboy hat strumming a guitar, a man with whistle, and a pelican, wings extended, readying itself for a nosedive.

I set down the paddle. Spread my arms wide. Lowered my eyelids and surrendered to the sway.

ACKNOWLEDGMENTS

My gratitude to all who helped make this book possible:

Critique partners: Marjorie Carlson Davis, Suzanne Kelsey, Claudia Bischoff, Jeannette Batko, Barbara Darling, Faith Gansheimer, and last, but not least, my sister-in-law, Sandy Daniels.

Of course I can't forget the Savvy Press gang for accepting me into their publication corral, especially Ellen Larson. Nor can I leave out my partner, Tom, who respects my need to write.

And, of course, hardy thanks to Miami author/blogger R.V. Reyes who read the book and wrote the back blurb.

This book could not have found a more phenomenal cover artist than Peg Cullen or jacket designer than Carrie Peters. To my Boston editor/proofreader, Betty Tyson, thank you is not enough.

During my journey, New York author and editor Lou Aronica inadvertently sent me on a learning path when he said: "You may not have the DNA to write a mystery." I thank him for providing that challenge. I just love a challenge.

To my family, my friends around the world. To those readers who continually asked when the next Jessie Murphy Mystery would be out. To the more than gracious business owners and locals of Matlacha who provide me inspiration for my work: Thank you.

ABOUT THE AUTHOR

jd lives and writes both in Florida and Iowa. She has also lived in the Boston area, Cambridge, England and In Ankara, Turkey. She holds a Doctor of Arts degree from Drake University and is an editor of Prairie Wolf Press Review, an online literary journal publishing established and emerging writers and visual artists.

She enjoys walking, kayaking, bicycling, playing tennis, bridge, and mahjong. Even more, she likes laughing and sharing stories with friends and family. She considers herself one lucky woman.

Please visit her website for further information and to contact her. www.live-from-jd.com

OTHER BOOKS BY THE AUTHOR

JESSIE MURPHY MYSTERIES

Through Pelican Eyes
Quick Walk to Murder

STAND-ALONE NOVELS

Minute of Darkness & Eighteen Flash
Fiction Stories

NONFICTION

The Old Wolf Lady: A Biography
(First Edition)
The Old Wolf Lady: Wawewa Mepemoa
(Second Edition)

POETRY

Currents that Puncture: A Dissertation
Say Yes